Women Without Men

Women Without Men

A NOVEL OF MODERN IRAN

Shahrnush Parsipur

Translated from the Persian
by Faridoun Farrokh

FOREWORD BY SHIRIN NESHAT

THE
FEMINIST PRESS
AT THE CITY UNIVERSITY
OF NEW YORK
NEW YORK CITY

Published in 2011 by the Feminist Press
at the City University of New York
The Graduate Center
365 Fifth Avenue, Suite 5406
New York, NY 10016

feministpress.org

Originally published in Persian as *Zanan bedoone mardan*
by Nashr-e Noqreh in 1989.

Zanan bedoone mardan copyright © 1989 by Shahrnush Parsipur
Translation copyright © 2011 by Faridoun Farrokh
Foreword copyright © 2011 by Shirin Neshat
Author's Note copyright © 2011 by Shahrnush Parsipur

NATIONAL
ENDOWMENT
FOR THE ARTS
A great nation
deserves great art.

This project is supported in part by an award from the
National Endowment for the Arts.

Fourth printing July 2023

Cover image: Feature film still from *Women Without Men* (2009)
by Shirin Neshat. Cover and text design by Drew Stevens.

Library of Congress Cataloging-in-Publication Data

Parsipur, Shahrnush.
  [Zanan bidun-i mardan. English]
  Women without men : a novel / by Shahrnush Parsipur ;
translation, Faridoun Farrokh.
    p. cm.
  ISBN 978-1-55861-753-7
  I. Farrokh, Faridoun. II. Title.
  PK6561.P247Z3613 2011
  891'.5533—dc23

                                    2011039846

Contents

Foreword

GABRIEL GARCIA MARQUEZ once defined magic realism as the way in which his grandmother told stories to
him; even when nothing made sense, he believed her
every word, first because she was his grandmother, second because she told her story with such conviction that
he didn't dare question her. In *Women Without Men*, Shahrnush Parsipur too becomes the master of ceremonies. She
creates her own universe where no outside rules apply.
She makes you believe the unbelievable with such ease,
subtlety, and grace that you don't dare doubt her. She
unleashes a dead woman and brings her back to life; she
plants another woman to grow as a tree; the men in a

brothel suddenly become headless; a woman gives birth to a flower and they fly off to the skies.

It's difficult to summarize my personal journey, the six years I spent in the process of adapting this magnificent and majestic novella into a feature film. This exhilarating and, at times, painful experience became my entry into Shahrnush's wild imagination. I was first drawn to this novella because of its visual, mystical, and allegorical force. Unlike in any other contemporary Iranian literature, Shahrnush's style of writing achieves a universal significance while remaining fully authentic to its local cultural context.

Essentially, I found that at its core, *Women Without Men* has a powerful and paradoxical arc that traverses various notions of opposites: magic/realism, nature/culture, local/universal, men/women, mystical/political. Shahrnush situates the city of Tehran as a point of entry to all sorts of cultural, sociopolitical, and historical realities, while the orchard functions purely on a metaphoric level. Not unlike the Garden of Eden, this orchard becomes a utopian island, a place of exile where women may take refuge, as long as they respect its rules. When in the city of Tehran, fully conscious of time and place, we delve into a specific country's cultural and collective political crisis. But once inside the orchard we abandon all logic of time and place, and face the deeply existential and personal crisis of a few women.

Adapting *Women Without Men* into a screenplay and balancing the allegorical versus the sociopolitical tendencies of the narrative proved to be a lengthy and complicated process. Together with Shoja Azari, and in consultation with Shahrnush herself, we discussed and analyzed the novella's characters, symbolic intentions, and narrative plots endlessly, and how we might best translate them into a film. We faced many barriers, including the fact that magic realism is notoriously difficult to turn into a screenplay. Among other obstacles were how to develop the stories of five main characters with equal importance into a single narrative. Each female protagonist was unique in her socioeconomic background, and emerged with a radically different emotional and moral predicament. Even more challenging, some of the characters were fully realistic while others were highly allegorical. So along the way, we had to make difficult decisions such as eliminating one of the characters, Mahdokht, who was the most magical protagonist among the women. (In 2003 I made a video installation devoted to Mahdokht). We also took other liberties and expanded the historical and political aspects of the narrative, most specifically the CIA-organized coup of 1953, which remains in the background in the novella.

But the difficulties didn't stop there. *Women Without Men* had been banned in Iran, and Shahrnush herself lived in exile. Therefore, we had to abandon the idea of shooting the film in our native country. We took on the challenge of recreating Tehran and Karadj in Casablanca, Morocco, where our wonderful team took meticulous care to bring Shahrnush's fantastic images to life and beautifully captured the life of Iran in the 1950s. Ultimately *Women Without Men* became a genuinely international effort—a

German, French, and Austrian production, directed by Iranians, and shot in Morocco.

Most important of all, this beautiful journey brought me the gift of deep friendship with Shahrnush Parsipur. Throughout the six years we worked together on the film, I often wondered whether my motivation behind making *Women Without Men* was due to my devotion to the novella or to Shahrnush herself. I have always taken inspiration from Iranian women writers, and have often inscribed some of these writers' texts onto my photographic images. But my encounter with Shahrnush touched me profoundly, not only on an artistic, but on a personal level. The more I learned about her, the more I idolized her, her courage, strength, and ability to endure the hardship that life had imposed on her. In many ways Shahrnush embodies her own characters' anguish and pain, as well as their will to transcend suffering. With *Women Without Men*, Shahrnush reaffirms the simple truth that fragility and strength live side by side, and these attributes are volatile, precious, and endlessly female.

Shirin Neshat
New York City

Women Without Men

Mahdokht

THE ORCHARD, VIBRANTLY GREEN and with adobe walls, backed up against the village at one end and bordered the river at the other. It was an orchard mostly of sweet and sour cherries. The villa, a mixture of rustic and urban architecture, sat in the middle of it. It had three rooms that looked onto a small reflecting pool, now green with algae and occupied by frogs. A gravel path flanked by willow trees surrounded the pool. In the afternoon the light green of the trees noiselessly competed with the dark green of the pool, a struggle that disturbed Mahdokht who had no tolerance for conflict of any kind and simply wished for a universal harmony, even among all shades of green in the world.

"It is a soothing color, but still . . ."

The bedstead was under one of the willows, two of its legs on the ledge of the pool. There was the possibility that they would slide off the slimy ledge, pulling the whole bedstead into the pool. In the afternoons Mahdokht would perch herself on this bed and contemplate not only the rivalry between the green of the trees and the pool water, but also the way the blue of the sky imposed itself, like the verdict of a divine judge, on the green of the orchard.

It was in the winter months that Mahdokht thought of engaging in knitting projects, or taking French lessons, or going on a guided world tour, because the winter air was pure and breathable. In the summer, on the other hand, the air was laden with smoke, dust, pollutants from cars and people, and a depressing feeling from large windowpanes unable to keep out the heat of the sun.

"Goddamn, why don't these people understand that those windows are no good in this climate?"

Such thoughts brought on a wave of sadness, making her prone to accepting the invitation from Houshang Khan, her elder brother, to join the family in the orchard where she had to tolerate the children who screamed all the time as they gorged themselves with cherries giving themselves diarrhea and eating yogurt at night as antidote.

"The yogurt is from the village," her brother would say to indicate its high quality.

"It's outstanding," she would concur.

The children always felt cold to the touch and looked

pale, although they ingested more food than appropriate for their age, and later "barfed," as their mother said.

Earlier on, when she was a teacher, Mr. Ehteshami would say, "Miss Parhami, please file this form there . . . Miss Parhami, ring the bell . . . Talk to this janitor, whose language I don't understand." As principal, Mr. Ehteshami seemed to enjoy having her as assistant principal. She did not mind the arrangement either. But then one day he turned to her and said, "Miss Parhami, Would you like to go to the cinema with me tonight? There is a good movie playing."

She went pale, not knowing how to deal with this forwardness. What did the little man think? Who did he think she was? What was his intention?

Now she understood why the female teachers suppressed their smiles and pursed their lips every time Mr. Ehteshami talked to her. They must have sensed something. But they were wrong about her. Now she would show them who she really was.

She quit the job without notice. However, when she heard a year later that Mr. Ehteshami had married Miss Atai, the history and geography teacher, she felt such a tightness in her chest as if her heart was about to burst out.

"My problem is that Father has left too much money behind."

That was the case. The next winter she knitted for the first two children of Houshang Khan. Ten years later she was knitting for five of them.

"I wonder why people produce so many children."

"I can't help it," returned Houshang Khan. "I love children."

Really, what could he do? He can't help it, she thought.

She had recently seen a movie with Julie Andrews in it. Julie's character had become involved with an Austrian man, the martinet father of seven children whom he ordered around by blowing a whistle. Julie had first intended to join a convent but had thought better of it and married the Austrian since she was expecting his eighth child, especially since the Nazis were marching on Austria and there were many uncertainties.

"I am as tender-hearted as Julie in the movie."

She was right. She wouldn't hurt a fly. Besides, she had fed four hungry dogs in the street and had given her brand-new topcoat to the school janitor. When she was a teacher, in compliance with the Public Centers Program, she had visited the orphanage three times, on each occasion she had taken several pounds of pastries for the children.

"What nice children!"

She wouldn't mind if some of them were her own. They would always have clean clothes and no snot running down their faces. They would also use the proper term to refer to the bathroom.

"I wonder what will become of them."

This was a tough question, especially since the state radio and television had made statements on the need to do something about them. Both Mahdokht and the state were concerned about the orphans. What if she had a thousand hands and could knit five hundred sweaters a week?

"Two hands per sweater," she figured, "so one thousand hands would equal five hundred sweaters."

But a person cannot have a thousand hands, especially Mahdokht, who loved the winter and took daily afternoon walks during the season. It would take five hours or so to put one thousand gloves on one thousand hands.

"No," she reasoned with herself, "with the first five hundred hands I would put gloves on the other five hundred hands and then repeat the process. Three minutes or less. That's all."

This is not the real problem. It is up to the government to set up a factory and produce sweaters as needed.

Mahdokht dipped her toes in the pool water.

The first day of her visit she waded in the river. The ice-cold water made her muscles ache. She immediately withdrew, fearing that she might catch a cold. She put on her socks and shoes and strolled toward the greenhouse. The door was open and a rush of muggy air greeted her. Several years ago Mr. Ehteshami had said that breathing greenhouse air is salutary as plants generate oxygen during the day. But that day there were no plants in the greenhouse as they had all been taken out to the orchard and planted in flowerbeds. She walked in the narrow passageway looking at the dusty panes of glass enclosing the greenhouse. She heard a struggle and heavy breathing, something feverish, hot, and scorching—and sensed the smell of bodies.

Her heart missed a beat. The servant girl, Fati, fifteen

years old, but more resembling a streetwalker, lay at the far end of the greenhouse with Yadollah, the gardener, with a bald head and repulsive, red-rimmed eyes, panting, panting, panting.

Mahdokht, near collapse and reaching for a shelf to steady herself, could not take her eyes off the scene. The man was the first to notice her. He let out a squeal and tried to disentangle himself from the embrace of the girl by hitting her in the face with one hand and reaching with the other for Mahdokht, who rushed out of the greenhouse and wandered aimlessly in the courtyard, fraught with nausea. She hurried to the pool, dipped her hands in the water, washing them compulsively. She then sat on the edge of the bedstead.

"What shall I do?"

She thought of reporting the whole thing to Houshang Khan and his wife. After all, the girl was in their custody.

"The girl is barely fifteen years old—what outrageous behavior . . ."

Houshang Khan would give her a sound beating before sending her back to her family. Most likely her brothers would kill her.

"What shall I do?"

Perhaps she should pack her bags and return to Tehran and leave behind the agonizing quandary.

"Then what?"

In a fit of indecision she walked back toward the greenhouse. She saw the girl, wearing her chador inside out, rushing toward her. Her face looked scratched and flushed.

"Dear madam," she whimpered, as she dropped to the ground hugging Mahdokht's feet.

The girl yelps like a dog, she thought.

"Get away from me, you filth," Mahdokht snapped.

"Oh no, please madam," pleaded the girl, "I'll do anything for you."

"Shut up. Let me pass."

"I swear I'll be your slave for life. I'll be as good as dead if you tell my mother."

"Who said I wanted to tell?"

"I swear to God he wants to marry me. He's going to see the master tomorrow to propose."

Reluctantly, Mahdokht promised not to tell simply to get away from her. She felt repulsed by the touch of the girl's hands on her ankles. Fati rose to her feet and stumbled unsteadily toward the building. Mahdokht drew a deep breath, suppressing an urge to cry.

Since then three months had passed and the summer was at an end. Preparations were being made for the family's return to the city that day. Everyone was surprised by Yadollah the gardener's sudden and unannounced departure. "That's weird," Houshang Khan had said. "He'd told me a hundred times he would never leave my service." Now he had to hire another caretaker to protect the orchard from the ravages of winter.

"Anybody can set up a maximum of four benches on the riverbank and rent them to Friday visitors for thirty tomans," Houshang Khan explained to an assembly of villagers, who listened respectfully and approvingly.

Mahdokht then heard the girl's hearty laughter. She had taken the children to the end of the orchard to keep them out of the way. "God knows what games she teaches them," she wondered, as she paced the floor angrily in her room, occasionally punching a wall in frustration. She worried about the children.

"I wish she had gotten pregnant so they would have killed her."

It would have been convenient if the girl had gotten pregnant. The brothers would have ganged up on her and beaten her to death. That would have been nice. Then she wouldn't mislead the children.

Suddenly and unaccountably a thought came to Mahdokht's mind: my virginity is like a tree.

She felt compelled to look at her face in the mirror.

"Perhaps that is why I am green."

She had an olive complexion with a hint of sallowness. There were wrinkles under her eyes. A vein tracked visibly on her forehead.

"You are so frigid," Mr. Ehteshami had once noted. "Like ice."

"Not like ice," she thought. "I am a tree."

She could plant herself in the earth.

"Well, I am not an acorn, but a tree. I should plant myself."

No way could she talk like that to Houshang Khan, telling him to sit down for a frank conversation, telling him that it was the factories that produced the sweaters. If she mentioned the sweaters, she would have to tell him about the thousand hands. He would never understand.

How could she tell him, for instance, that with the factories producing thousands of sweaters, there would be no need for her to be trained and oriented as a knitter?

Well, there was no choice. She contemplated staying behind and planting herself when the winter came. She should have asked the arborists as to the best time to plant saplings. She didn't really know. It didn't matter. She would stay for the planting. From a sapling she would grow into a tree. She wanted to be planted near the river and grow leaves darker than algae so she could seriously challenge the water of the pool. As a tree she would sprout offshoots that would spread to the entire orchard and cover it so thickly that they would have to cut down all the cherry trees to make room for the Mahdokht tree. Soon it would spread to the rest of the continent. Americans would buy shoots of it to plant in California and colder climates, although they would mispronounce it "Madokt." Soon, as a result of widespread usage in other languages, the name would be corrupted to "Medok" or "Madok." Four centuries from now etymologists would passionately argue that both terms share the same root, "Madik," and it was originally from Africa. The botanists on the other hand would raise objections that a cold-climate tree could not grow in Africa.

Mahdokht beat her head against the wall repeatedly. She broke down and started crying. As she sobbed violently, she thought that she would take a tour of Africa. She wanted to be a tropical tree. This was what she wanted with all her heart. It is always the heart's desire that drives one insane.

Fa'iza

AFTER SEVERAL DAYS OF DOUBT and hesitation Fa'iza made up her mind at four in the afternoon on August 5, 1953. Silence was no longer feasible. If she waited any longer everything would collapse. She'd better stand up in her own defense. Even so, despite the fact that she felt empowered by the decision, it took her well over an hour to get dressed. Slowly and deliberately she put on her stockings, a blouse, and a lightweight cotton skirt. During the process she paused to think, what if Amir Khan is there. The thought sent a rush of heat through her body. With him around, she wouldn't be able to say what she wanted, or say anything at all. She would have to hold back and endlessly revise what she was going to say.

"I'm aging," she told herself as she stood in front of the mirror powdering her nose. At twenty-eight years and two months she was not old; she just looked prematurely aged.

She put on her shoes and picked up a handbag before going downstairs. Nana Jan, her ancient grandmother, was sitting on a bench gazing at the reflecting pool in the middle of the courtyard. The clacking of Fa'iza's heels on the steps distracted her.

"Are you going out?" she asked.

"Yes."

"Not a good idea. Demonstrations everywhere."

The neighbors had the radio on and the noise reached the courtyard. Fa'iza stopped momentarily. Nana Jan was right.

"At least wear a chador," advised Nana Jan.

Wordlessly Fa'iza turned around and went upstairs. From under piles of clothing she brought out the black chador she wore at funerals and on religious occasions. She put it on. The heavy folds of the material made her look somewhat angular. Amir Khan would tease her, should he be there. She didn't mind being teased by him most of the time, for instance, for her inability to find a husband, but not for looking the way she did in a chador. That would likely make her cry—not a wise thing to do in front of Amir Khan. Any way, she had no choice, so she went downstairs wearing the chador. Nana Jan made no more comments; it had been a while since she'd stopped bossing people around.

Fa'iza stepped outside into the side street. The noise

of the demonstration in the distance was clearly audible. A taxicab arrived almost immediately.

"Sezavar Street," she said as she got in.

The driver looked at her in the rearview mirror.

"Aren't you scared?" he asked. "It is chaotic out there."

"I have no choice."

"I have to take detours, you know," the driver said. "Main streets are dangerous."

"No problem," Fa'iza answered.

Through a maze of back streets and alleys the driver negotiated his way until he had to stop at a minor traffic jam at an intersection. In the middle of the intersection a man appeared to be directing traffic. But all of a sudden he left the spot and ran down the sidewalk into an alley, chased by another man. The traffic began to move slowly. Suddenly a man hurled himself onto the back of Fa'iza's cab and started knocking on the rear window with a knife. Fa'iza turned her head and buried her face in her lap. The driver jammed on the brakes, making her lurch forward and hit her head against the front seat. He then accelerated, which threw Fa'iza violently against the back seat. The maneuver made the man slip off the trunk of the car.

"I told you it would be dangerous," said the driver. "You're my last fare for sure." Fa'iza made no response.

"Goddamn!" exclaimed the driver, "Serves me right for being nosy! My old lady told me ten times not to get on the road today."

Fa'iza remained silent. She didn't like the way the driver looked at her in the rearview mirror. She was anxious to get out.

Finally they arrived at the destination. She put a two-toman bill in the driver's outstretched hand, shuddering at the touch of his skin. Not waiting for the change, she burst out of the cab.

The house overlooked the street, which was humming with the noise of the crowds at some distance. Fa'iza rang the doorbell. She had a bitter taste in her mouth for the two minutes before the door was opened. The maid, Alia, opened the door, looking groggy.

"You were still asleep?" said Fa'iza accusingly. "My God!"

Alia muttered something by way of greeting and stepped aside to let Fa'iza in.

"Is Madam Munis home?" Fa'iza asked.

"Yes."

"Where?"

"In the living room, I suppose."

Fa'iza started in that direction. Would Amir Khan be there, she wondered. As she took the first step, she told herself "There," and with the second step, "Not there." She alternated the thoughts at each step until she reached the living room door, coinciding with "There." Apprehensively she pushed open the door. Munis was by herself sitting in front of the radio listening intently. Amir Khan was not there. He might be asleep upstairs, she guessed.

"Hello!" Fa'iza exclaimed.

Munis turned, her face suddenly flushed with pleasure at the sight of Fa'iza. "What a surprise," she squealed. "Long time no see! Where have you been hiding yourself, young lady?" Slowly she rose to her feet, turning down the volume on the radio.

"Long-time-no-see to you, my dear," returned Fa'iza. "No word, no message, for God's sake." The women embraced and continued the stream of pleasantries as they settled on a couch next to the radio.

"Are you alone?" Fa'iza wanted to know.

"Yes, I am," declared Munis. "Mother and the others have gone on a pilgrimage to Mashad."*

"Why didn't you let me know?" Fa'iza asked, complainingly.

"They've been gone two days."

"I see. What is Amir Khan doing?"

"He's not home. He is at work."

"What? At work? In the middle of all this commotion?"

"Every time he leaves the house he says he is going to the office. What do I know?"

"That's interesting."

"Interesting is the way you are."

"I take it as a compliment."

"I'm not sure about that," said Munis with a touch of playfulness. "Would you like some tea?"

"That would be nice. If it's not too much trouble."

As soon as Munis left to get the tea, Fa'iza turned off the radio. It could interfere with the conversation that she had delayed long enough. When she returned, Munis sat directly across from Fa'iza, not saying a word. Somewhere Fa'iza had read that people with round faces are mentally

---

* A holy city in northeastern Iran where the eighth imam in the Shiite tradition is buried.

defective. She had run to the mirror to make sure she did not belong to this retarded group, although she had been made aware many times before, mostly by Nana Jan's pejorative, hurtful comments, that she had horse-like features. Since she'd read this, Fa'iza had developed the habit of evaluating people based on the shape of their faces. Amir had decidedly an oblong face with a strong, square jaw. Munis, on the other hand, had a round face, like the full moon, or an egg. For the past ten years she had thought of Munis as an imbecile. Fa'iza had cultivated a friendship with her despite the fact that Munis was ten years her senior because she found in her a winsome sincerity and personal magnetism. A couple of years after their bonding as friends, Munis's brother, Amir, entered the picture. Now, every time she paid Munis a visit, it was mostly in hopes of catching a glimpse of Amir Khan. If Munis had had a longer face, Fa'iza had speculated often, she would have been smart enough to arrange Fa'iza's marriage to Amir Khan. Poor girl, Fa'iza thought to herself, why is her face so round?

Alia brought in the tea tray. As they sipped tea, Munis kept glancing at the radio. Although she was older and in her own house, she did not have the self-confidence to exert her will and turn the radio back on. "Is it bad out there?" she asked.

"It is utterly chaotic," Fa'iza answered.

"Amir Khan warned me not leave the house. He said I might get my head cut off."

"Well, he is right. Someone jumped on the trunk of my cab," Fa'iza added.

Thinking that she should focus the conversation on her intended topic, she immediately asked "Have you seen Parveen lately?"

"I haven't seen her in a month," answered Munis.

"Well, why not?"

"The last time I saw her was when her child was sick with rubella. She told people to stay away to avoid spreading the virus."

"Just as well you didn't see more of her."

Munis looked at her companion quizzically. Fa'iza waited for her to pick up the thread of the conversation, but the older woman remained silent, staring at the patterns on the rug. So Fa'iza had to continue.

"Never in my life have I seen such an indecent person," Fa'iza blurted.

Munis lifted her head and looked at her with eyes awash in surprise. "But why?" she asked in bewilderment.

Oh, God, I wish her face wasn't so round, Faiza thought to herself.

"She's mean and vicious," she said venomously. "It is terrible to find this out about a person you have been friends with for fifteen years. She's all pretense and not an ounce of sincerity in her."

There was something close to fear in Munis's eyes as she asked, "What has she done? Sued for divorce?"

"Oh no. What divorce?" Fa'iza hissed. "That is the last thing she'd do, that filth. My poor brother is wasted on her."

Munis pursed her lips, completely absorbed. In her mind she was trying unsuccessfully to find a reason for such a view of Parveen. She had known the woman through Fa'iza at parties, funerals, and other such functions and had come to have a casual friendship with her. She'd never detected any serious flaws in her character.

Munis stared at Fa'iza, expecting an explanation. Fa'iza returned her gaze, her eyes turning red. Suddenly she began to cry. This evoked a sympathetic response in Munis who started sobbing uncontrollably. She had always had a tendency to cry at the sight of other people's tears. She never knew why.

"Don't cry," Munis pleaded. "Oh, please don't cry for God's sake. What is the matter?"

Fa'iza was looking for a handkerchief, and not finding one dabbed her eyes with the corner of her chador, now fallen in a heap around her.

"Do you know how nice I was to her?" Fa'iza asked, not waiting for an answer. "She wouldn't be so fortunate had it not been for me. It was just this past year when she had a row with my brother. It was her fault. The stupid woman packed up and ran to her mommy's. No decent woman with a lick of sense would do such a thing. And who do you think patched things up between them? Poor me! I gave a dinner party that is still being talked about all over town. I went to the best meat market and tipped the butcher for extra-fine cuts of meat. I made eggplant stew with lamb and rice. And grilled chicken. What a grilled chicken! I marinated it in lemon juice and spices and spent a whole hour roasting it on an open fire in the courtyard. I made yogurt and spinach. Do you think it was easy to find tomatoes out of season? I went all the way to the farmer's market to get them. I had Colonel Sarvbala's orderly get enough vodka for Parveen's father to drink all night."

As if to keep down the bitterness welling up inside her, Fa'iza pressed her lips together. Munis was looking at Fa'iza, her eyes bulging. "Then what?" she asked.

"What do you think? It was like another wedding." Fa'iza said with a shrug of her shoulders. "My brother took her back. Then two months later she supposedly wanted to reciprocate, but actually the bitch wanted to outdo me and make me look bad. She gave a dinner party serving a European menu. She threw a few pieces of shoe leather on a china plate calling them steaks, like we are peasants, like we have no taste. I knew right away that she wanted to antagonize me. All right, I said to myself, you want war, I'll show you war!"

"She never told me she was at war with anyone," Munis muttered , trying not to sound defiant.

"What do you think she could say?" Fa'iza retorted. "Could she say she was trying to upstage me? All these years those who have tasted my cooking have had nothing but compliments. How could this upstart go around challenging me? She is just malicious by nature."

"I see," Munis said resignedly.

"Well," Fa'iza continued, "I went and got myself a cookbook. If I can make the rice and lamb dish the way I do, I can make steaks out of a rubber mat. I learned all about it."

"I'm sure," said Munis in confirmation. "It is not a big

deal. There is a cooking show on the radio every morning. It makes it sound so simple."

"That is exactly what I was trying to prove. So I gave another dinner party," Fa'iza said with a touch of self-satisfaction.

"When was that?" Munis asked.

"Just about a month ago," Fa'iza replied. "I invited the same group to dinner with a European menu. I went to the meat market and tipped the butcher five tomans for eight prime-cut filets. I bought green beans. I bought snow peas. I bought tomatoes and small potatoes. I mixed rice with beans for the salad. I also made yogurt and spinach. The sauce I made for the filets was delicious. From the fruit stalls downtown I bought the largest peaches and nectarines, as well as sweet and sour cherries. I asked Colonel Sarvbala's orderly to get me the best vodka again. I poured it into a decanter. I put some ice in Grandma's crystal fruit bowl and put the decanter in the middle of it."

Munis was fascinated, staring at Fa'iza admiringly. "Why did you do that?" she wanted to know.

"To keep the vodka chilled," Fa'iza replied triumphantly.

"Wow!"

"I wish you were there to see."

"Why didn't you invite me?"

"Well, Amir Khan was in Shiraz and you couldn't get back home alone late at night."

"I see," said Munis, somewhat crestfallen.

"What can I say, they just ate and ate and gave me compliment after compliment. The little bitch was bursting with jealousy. She'd turned red like a slice of beet."

"You mean Parveen?" Munis asked, somewhat perplexed.

"Of course. Who else?" answered Fa'iza. "You know what she did then?" Not waiting for an answer, Fa'iza continued, "Without warning she turned to me and said 'Foozy dear'—giving me a nickname, 'Foozy,' as if she couldn't bring herself to call me by my full name—'Foozy dear, let me tell you something. You don't put sauce on filet mignon.' She said it so loud the whole neighborhood could hear."

"Really!"

"You can't guess how that made me feel. 'Who says you don't put sauce on filet mignon?' I asked. She said she'd heard it on the radio. I said I have read the instruction in a book. She said she'd also read it in a book. I said the book she read must have been garbage. At this point my brother intervened and said with or without sauce it was just delicious. The little woman blew up like a balloon because my brother had taken my side, and she continued to sulk through dinner."

By now Munis was so engrossed in the account that Fa'iza felt she had to add a few more embellishments to her narrative.

"She acted uptight until the men went on the balcony," Fa'iza went on. "She stayed behind supposedly to help me clear the table."

Fa'iza went silent, her lips pressed tight and tears streaming down her cheeks, as if in anticipation of the enormity of what she was about to relate.

"Oh, God. Please don't cry," Munis implored, her tears flowing.

"Then," Fa'iza went on, "the bitch turned to me and said 'A woman who messes around with Fetty in the hall should think more of protecting her virginity curtain than throwing dinner parties.'" By now tears were streaming down Fa'iza's face to her lap. Munis, equally tearful, asked, "Who is Fetty?"

"That son-of-a-bitch, her brother," Fa'iza answered. "He looks like shit, like a overflowing toilet. I was outraged. I thought of slapping her so hard to burst her eardrums, something she'd never forget. But for better or worse my brother was nearby and I thought better of it. But if she was taunting me, I'd taunt her back. 'First of all,' I told her, 'only the Angel of Death would mess around with your brother. The way he looks only the Angel of Death would be interested in him. Secondly, virginity is not a curtain; it's an orifice, and you wouldn't know the difference after three kids. And you go around talking behind people's back.'"

Munis had ceased crying. With her mouth open, she was staring at Fa'iza, who continued to talk after a short pause. "I told her if she opened her filthy mouth once again and talked like she did I'd teach her a lesson she'd remember for life. Good thing she is afraid of my brother, who was nearby. So she shut her trap."

Without a word, Munis stared at the floral patterns on the carpet. Fa'iza, as she dried her eyes, intently watched the expression on her face.

"I know she is a snake," Fa'iza said, "and won't let go until she injects her venom. Now she is going around bad-mouthing me. But I don't care. My conscience is clear. I was so incensed I wanted to get a virginity certificate from the midwife and frame it on the wall for all to see."

Munis continued to stare at the rug.

"According to my mother," Munis said softly, "the hymen is a membrane that can rip open, even if a girl falls from a height."

"What talk is that?" Fa'iza said dismissively. "It's an orifice. It is constricted and it will expand as a result of penetration."

"Oh!" exclaimed Munis, the color draining from her face. Alarmed, Fa'iza asked, "Something's the matter?"

"No, no, it's nothing. But it must be a membrane," Munis insisted.

"No, dear woman," Fa'iza said emphatically. "I have read it in a book. I read a lot, you know. It is an orifice."

Carrying a fruit tray, Alia entered the room, followed almost immediately by Amir Khan. Fa'iza acknowledged him demurely. The squarely built man made himself comfortable in an armchair in the corner of the room as he greeted the women.

"It is really crazy out there," he said. "Don't plan on going out."

He noticed the women's red eyes. "What's wrong?" he asked.

"Nothing," said Munis.

Not satisfied with the answer, he asked more firmly, "I'm asking, what is the matter?"

"We were just having a girl talk," said Fa'iza, trying to lighten the mood.

"Why are you crying?" He wanted to know.

"Well, we're women, you know."

This brought a faint smile to his lips.

"I must get going," said Fa'iza.

"Where to? It's total chaos outside. It's so bad a dog wouldn't recognize its master," said Amir Khan.

"It is not that bad," Fa'iza ventured.

Amir Khan did not appreciate being contradicted. "On principle," he said, "women belong in the house. The outside is the world of men."

Fa'iza made no response. It was no use arguing with Amir Khan. Better wait for time to do its work. Now that she'd put the matter with Parveen to rest, the woman could no longer muddy the waters. She was happy with herself for having taken the initiative.

Amir Khan stood up, preparing to take Fa'iza home before daylight faded. Fa'iza was secretly delighted to have time alone with him.

"It will be safer if we take the side streets," she said. "That's what the cab driver told me."

Munis

Part One: Death

AT FOUR O'CLOCK IN THE AFTERNOON on August 7, 1953, Munis was standing on the roof of the house watching the street below. She had not slept a wink for exactly fifty-six hours. Amir Khan had forbidden her to leave the house.

From the roof she watched the street thick with crowds that seemed to be running back and forth, as if chasing each other. Then a convoy of trucks packed with people went by, followed by a procession of tanks. The sound of machine-gun fire could be heard from a distance.

Munis was thinking obsessively that for as long as she could remember she had looked at the garden through the window convinced that virginity was a delicate, vulnerable membrane. At the age of eight she had been told that God would not forgive a girl who lost her virginity in any way. Now, a couple of days ago she had learned that virginity was not a curtain but an orifice. Something had broken inside her and a cold rage penetrated her body. She thought of her childhood days when she had longingly looked at hedges and trees, hoping for a time in her life when she could freely climb them without compromising her virginity. Her knees felt like ice.

"I'll take my revenge," she told herself.

A man turned into the alley on the side of the house. He moved unsteadily with his hand pressing on his belly. He came a few steps into the alley and fell in the ditch head first. From where she was Munis could not see his face but his feet were sticking out of the ditch.

Munis closed her eyes and leaned forward. Within five seconds she was plastered on the pavement below, face up, eyes open, staring at the blue of the sky.

Munis

Part Two: Birth and Dying Again

AT FIRST MUNIS WAS DEAD. Or at least she thought she was. For the longest time she lay on the pavement, her eyes wide open. Gradually the blue of the sky darkened and tears began to flow down her face. She pressed on her eyes with her right hand and slowly rose to her feet. Her body felt sore and very weak.

Farther down the alley a man had fallen into a ditch with his legs sticking out. Uncontrollably Munis moved in his direction. The man's face was also turned skyward, his eyes open.

"Are you all right?" Munis asked.

"I'm dead," the man answered.

"Can I help you in any way?"

"The best thing for you to do is to leave. You might get into trouble."

"Why?"

"Can't you hear the noise? It is payback time."

"So what are you doing here?" Munis wanted to know.

"Dear lady," said the man, with a touch of impatience, "I told you. I am dead."

Undeterred, Munis continued, "Now, if I nurse you and take care of you it is possible that you might revive."

"No," said the man, "it won't work anymore. A Frenchman has written a film script titled 'It Is Too Late.' I am at that stage. It is too late for me."

A wave of sadness washed over Munis. "In any case, perhaps . . ." she said hopefully. But the man curtly interrupted her. "I told you to go away," he said, visibly irritated. "This is ridiculous."

So Munis left the scene, and for a month wandered in the city streets. At first the streets were crowded with mobs fighting and killing one another. But the chaos subsided gradually and people returned to their homes, perhaps to reflect on the events with pangs of regret. Some ended up in prison and others found reasons to celebrate and engage in binge drinking at parties. Munis, no longer young, had no taste for such parties but watched the celebrants through the windows and heard the sound of their laughter. Few people ventured out at night because of the curfew, and patrol units stopping passersby asking for passwords. By and by Munis reached the bookstores across from the university. Sheepishly she looked at the covers of the books in the window without permitting herself to read their titles. But eventually she overcame her aversion and began to read them. She was intrigued by one book, which happened to be not in the store window but offered by a street vendor. Its title was *Sexual Fulfillment or How to Know Our Bodies*.

For twelve days Munis kept passing by the book vendor's cart, each time furtively glancing at the book and its title. On the thirteenth day she finally gathered up enough courage to approach the vendor.

"How much is this?" she asked.

"Five tomans," answered the man. She bought the book and found a deserted street where she sat in the shade of a tree and began reading. Without interruption she read the book cover to cover three times. Three days passed. At the end of the third day she looked up from the book. She saw the external world in a different light. She felt she had undergone a process of growth and maturation.

She discarded the book in the gutter and started walking, heading toward her house. She arrived home at sunset. Alia answered the doorbell. At the sight of Munis she gave a loud squeal and sank to her knees.

"Alia dear, what is the matter?" Munis asked as she helped the maid to her feet.

"Madam, you've given us quite a scare," exclaimed the maid. "For a whole month your parents and your brother have scoured the town and country looking for you. They cry tears of blood nightly. Where have you been? What have you been doing?"

Munis said nothing. She only shook her head and smiled knowingly. "Alia dear," she said after a long pause,

"I am not the old Munis anymore. I now know a lot more." She then walked calmly and resolutely to the living room. She sat in a chair in a corner, deep in thought.

Fifteen minutes later Amir Khan arrived home, looking harassed and disheveled. He froze momentarily at the sight of Munis in the living room.

"You shameless woman," he yelled, "where the hell have you been?"

Munis smiled benignly at her brother, unable to see a cause for outrage. She was not offended by the outburst. Nor was she surprised.

"You have ruined the family reputation," Amir Khan hissed viciously. "Up and down the neighborhood everyone knows that you've gone missing."

"I only went for a short walk," replied Munis, somewhat sarcastically. "With your permission, of course."

"You knew you were not supposed to go out during the riots, you slut," said Amir Khan, as he removed the belt from his waist and started beating Munis with it. For her part, Munis was taken aback by the violent outburst and suffered the strokes wordlessly without putting up a defense.

"Why are you beating me?" she said finally. "Are you a sadist?"

The words exacerbated Amir Khan's fury. He reached for the knife on the dining table and plunged it forcefully in her chest.

With a faint sigh the spinster died for a second time.

Munis

Part Three: The Rebirth

ALIA, HEARING THE SOUND of loud voices, entered the room. At the sight of Munis's blood-spattered body and a bloody knife in Amir Khan's hand, she screamed and fell to the floor in a swoon. By now Amir Khan had regained his composure enough to feel apprehensive. He gazed at the knife as if surprised to find it in his hand. Hurriedly, he put it on the table. But he changed his mind and picked it up. With a handkerchief that he produced from his pocket he wiped off his fingerprints from its handle and put it back on the table.

The doorbell rang and Amir Khan rushed to open it. His parents entered the hall. "We've checked with three police stations," they blurted out without waiting for Amir Khan to say a word. "No sign of her yet."

They proceeded to the living room, almost stumbling on Alia, still stretched on the floor, before noticing Munis's body. They looked at each other in total confusion. Almost in unison, they each gave a short, high-pitched scream and fainted, slumping to the floor.

Now here was Amir Khan with four motionless bodies at his feet. "Oh God, what am I to do?" he wondered aloud. He sat on the edge of a chair, staring at the scene before him. Gripped by despair, he began to sob. With the handkerchief in his hand he tried to dry his tears, only to notice that he had smeared his face with the blood on the handkerchief. With a shudder of disgust he threw it on the table and returned his gaze to the bodies on the floor that showed no sign of regaining consciousness. He was overcome with a sense of guilt.

The doorbell rang.

Because the family had contacted so many police stations on account of Munis's disappearance, it was not unusual for five or six agents and detectives to stop by on a daily basis for updates on the search. Amir Khan lunged toward the door and yanked it open intent on turning himself in.

It was Fa'iza. In the darkness of the hall she could not see Amir Khan's face clearly. "Hello," she said.

"Oh my goodness!" she exclaimed fearfully when Amir Khan stepped back into the light. She leaned against the wall.

"For God's sake," implored Amir Khan, "don't *you* go and faint on me too."

"I just came to see if there is any news on Munis," Fa'iza said, her voice trembling. Amir Khan pointed his finger in the direction of the living room.

Fa'iza opened the door and looked inside. She turned quickly and faced Amir Khan, all color drained from her face.

"Did you kill all of them?" she asked.

"No," answered Amir Khan, "only Munis."

"What are you going to do now?"

"I have no idea," replied Amir Khan, as he slid down the wall and squatted on the floor. He broke down crying helplessly. The sight of the despondent man gave Fa'iza the notion that fate had finally put her on the highway of life. She took off her chador and tossed it in a corner and crouched directly in front of Amir Khan.

"Man, listen to me," she addressed Amir Khan firmly. "This is an abomination. Why are you crying? You are a brother. You have honor, and a duty to protect it. You killed her? You did the right thing. Why not? She'd been gadding about for a whole month. No decent girl behaves like that. She was as good as dead. I'd do the same if I were you. Your mother has raised you nobly . . ." Fa'iza paused to produce a handkerchief from her bosom and give it to him to wipe off his tears.

Amir Khan, now calmer and more self-possessed, blew his nose in the handkerchief. Fa'iza's tirade was exactly the kind of consolation he needed and it had arrived as if through divine intervention. At the same time he thought it was unbecoming of a woman to keep a handkerchief between her breasts and squat before a man in a way that exposed her crotch. For a fleeting moment he thought that if Fa'iza had been his sister, he would have killed her for such indiscretion. But of course she was not his sister and her conduct was not of his concern. Besides, she was the source of consolation and reassurance that he most needed under the circumstances.

"In your opinion, what do we do now?" Amir Khan asked, sighing deeply.

"Well, we will bury her in the backyard," Fa'iza answered. "Nobody will be any the wiser. Lots of people get lost everyday and the coroner's office is too busy to come asking questions."

This sounded sensible to Amir Khan. He nodded his agreement and the two of them went to the yard. With a pickaxe and a shovel they had soon dug a shallow grave about three feet deep.

They returned to the living room where Alia and Amir Khan's parents were still prostrate on the floor, unconscious. The man and the woman carried Munis's body to the yard, placed it in the grave, and covered it with dirt. They then went back to the living room to clean the blood stains and obliterate any evidence of the crime.

A little later, Alia and the parents showed signs of coming to. Slowly they regained consciousness. However, because of the shock of the preceding events, they had no recollection of what had happened, except for Alia, who had a vague memory of having seen a corpse on the floor. But because she was illiterate, and a housemaid, she could not allow herself to express her thoughts. Furthermore, there was a rumor that Alia had a doppelganger who mischievously haunted the rooftops during the summer and peeped in tents where people slept. She made a decision not to raise any questions.

Amir Khan's mother was delighted to see Fa'iza. "My dear girl," she said effusively. "How are you? How nice to see you after so long!"

"What do you mean *so long*? I am always here imposing on your hospitality," answered Fa'iza.

"Nonesense! You're always welcome."

"I just stopped by to see if there is any news of Munis."

"Oh, my dear, she has not been found yet. My poor child! God willing, we'll find her."

"Very well, then. I'll make myself scarce. For God's sake, let me know as soon as you hear anything," Fai'za said as she prepared to leave.

"I am not going to let you leave. You have to stay for dinner," said the old woman emphatically. "Alia, go to the kitchen," she ordered.

"I really shouldn't bother you any longer," Fa'iza demurred.

"No bother at all. You're not leaving."

The issue was settled and Alia headed for the kitchen. As was her habit, she began singing softly, plaintively, a folk song from the western provinces while she cooked. The lyrics, in quatrains, described the poet's desire to be able to write and narrate the misery, the heartache, he felt in separation from his beloved.

After dinner, Amir Khan offered to drive Fa'iza home. In the car he was quiet and in a pensive mood. Fa'iza felt at ease enough to reach out and stroke his hand gripping the wheel. He showed no reaction.

"You know, after all this you should get married to put Munis's disappearance behind us," Fa'iza felt confident enough to suggest. "Besides," she went on, "you need a wife to be your companion and confidante, to take care of you and give you solace and comfort."

"Exactly!" said Amir Khan, with the force of an epiphany. "You are absolutely right."

A few days later Amir Khan spoke with his mother. "Mother," he began, perched nervously on the edge of a chair, "it may not be proper to talk about this under the circumstances, but I have been thinking for a while, and I have come to believe that I need a wife to be my companion and confidante, to take care of me and give me solace and comfort. That is why I have decided to get married."

"Oh, wonderful!" said the mother, genuinely delighted. "Of course, your poor sister is still missing. It would have been so much nicer if she could be a part of this auspicious occasion. But what can we do? God willing, when and where do you plan to have the wedding?"

"Well," said Amir Khan timidly, "first we must go through the marriage proposal phase."

"But aren't you going to marry Fa'iza?" she asked, somewhat confused.

"No, mother," he replied, "I intend to marry the daughter of Haji Mohammed Sorkhchehreh. She is eighteen years old and exceedingly pretty. She is bashful, caring, dutiful, chaste, and modest. She dresses and behaves properly in public. In the street she always walks with her head down. Please do me the favor of asking her hand in marriage on my behalf."

"Amir dear," the mother said, with some concern in her voice, "you are in fact two years older than your late sister and pushing forty. You did not get married so that you could take care of your sister. Now why do you want to marry an eighteen-year-old? You know the old saw, a young wife always attracts the neighbors. You may be asking for scandals."

Amir was adamant. "But mother," he said, "you've also heard the other saying: 'A virgin past twenty, pity she needs aplenty.' I have no choice but to marry someone below twenty. Besides, she looks very chaste and devout and not likely to be unfaithful. So why don't you dress up and go for the proposal today?"

Early in the afternoon the mother put on her most elaborate outfit, wrapped herself in a chador and, accompanied by Amir, left for the residence of the future bride. The girl, dressed conservatively in head cover and thick stockings, brought in the tea tray and offered it demurely to the visitors.

Amir's mother liked the prospective bride. The prospective bride liked the future mother-in-law. The groom's family approved of the bride's family, and the bride's family liked the groom's family. A date was set for the nuptials to take place the following Wednesday since the holy period of religious observances were at hand and could delay the ceremony by two months. The payment in the event of a divorce was set at fifteen thousand tomans. It was agreed that Amir Khan would provide the wherewithal for the ceremony, and that the reception would be held in the garden of the bride's residence—which happened to be more spacious and elegant than Amir's.

The mother and son returned home elated. They broke the news to Alia. For her part, she smiled knowingly and proceeded to slip out of the house on her way to see Fa'iza. When Alia told her about the development, the jilted woman beat her head against the wall and put her fist through the windowpane causing a gash on her knuckles. At Alia's suggestion she put on her chador and together they left for the shrine of Shah-Abolazim. At the altar Fa'iza lit twelve candles and vowed the charitable donation of a sheep for the intervention of holy spirits and the disruption of the marriage.

The two women then headed for Darvazeh Ghar to consult with Mirza Managhebi, the medium, and paid for a charm to avert the formation of affection between Amir Khan and his bethrothed. From there they hastened to the hamlet of Evrin to see Madam Baji, a well-known psychic. She was known for her pure spirit enabling her to see into the future by consulting an ancient, sacred book. She gazed momentarily at Fa'iza and opened the huge tome at a random page.

"The subject of this augury," she read from the page, "is a virgin of average height and weight, pleasant olive complexion, square face, small eyes, and ruby-red lips." Fa'iza was amazed at the accurate description of herself.

"She bears a sorrow," the psychic continued, "a sorrow of love. May God have mercy upon her." Fa'iza shook her head in affirmation, feeling a strong bond with the old, heavily wrinkled woman.

"To remove this burden of love," the old woman croaked, "the virgin must for seven nights take seven steps in the direction of Mecca and then retrace her steps and intone with each step, 'Dear God, protect me from satanic temptations.' She should then wash her feet before going to bed and leave her feet uncovered by the bedclothes."

"But madam," Fa'iza protested, "I am in love and I wish for union with my beloved. Give me a talisman or cast a spell to implant my love in the heart of this man."

"My dear girl," chuckled the old woman, "affairs of the heart cannot be forced. You must dispel this love. As ancient wisdom holds, 'Blissful as shared love can be, unrequited love is naught but unremitting heartache.'"

Frustrated, Fa'iza left the room in a huff, contemptuously throwing down a small coin at the old woman's feet. Madam Baji smiled knowingly, picked up the coin, and dropped it in an earthen piggy bank, perhaps thinking of it as a contribution toward her granddaughter's dowry.

Fa'iza faithfully performed the suggested ritual for seven nights as she moaned, wept, and growled with frustration. She toyed with the idea of going to the police with the whole story. She even thought of killing Amir Khan in retaliation for the murder of his sister. None of these options felt satisfying. Finally she decided to go to Munis's burial site on the night of the wedding and bury the love-destroying charm at the foot of the grave, hoping that the conflation of the victim's blood and the powers of the charm would afflict Amir Khan in some way.

Counting on help from Alia, who already suspected foul play in the disappearance of Munis, Fa'iza went to the deserted house on the wedding night. Alia let her in and then left to join the wedding party. Fa'iza went directly to the gravesite and in the gathering darkness began to dig a hole to bury the talisman.

Her blood curdled when she heard a soft voice calling her name. She looked around for the source and found none. The voice was unmistakably like that of Munis except that it sounded muffled, as if coming from the bottom of a well. Fa'iza swallowed hard and pressed her hand over her heart as if to keep it from bursting out of her chest. In a few moments she regained some of her composure only to hear the voice again. "Fa'iza dear, I can't breathe," it said.

Fa'iza made no response.

"I'm very hungry. I'm dying of thirst," she heard the voice say. "I haven't had anything to eat for a long time."

Reflexively and feverishly Fa'iza began to claw at the dirt, digging into the grave. She stopped when Munis's round face was exposed. The eyes opened and the lips began to move. "Dear sister, give me a little water."

Fa'iza rushed to the pool in the middle of the yard and in her cupped hands carried some water to the grave. She splashed it on the face and resumed digging with her fingers until Munis's whole body was uncovered and she made an effort to rise. Fa'iza helped her up and began to shake the dirt off the clothing. Slowly and unsteadily Munis moved in the direction of the house. By now Fa'iza had overcome her initial shock, although she did not know what to make of the situation. She followed Munis closely. Munis went straight to the kitchen and brought out a pot of leftovers. With muddy fingers she began to stuff her mouth with food. She had eaten almost half of what was in the pot before she was on the move again, staggering back to the yard. She went to the pump and drew a bucketful of stagnant water from the underground reservoir and gulped it down breathlessly.

For a moment she remained motionless in the darkness. She began to take off her clothes, making grunting sounds. She then jumped in the pool and proceeded to scrub her body vigorously. Meanwhile Fa'iza ran back to Munis's room, which the family had left untouched, and hunted for some towels and clothing, bringing them back to the side of the pool. Munis, panting with the exertion, dried herself, put on the clothes, and walked slowly but steadily to the living room slumping into her favorite chair next to the radio. Fa'iza, still dazed and in the grip of fear, sat in another chair facing Munis, who initiated a conversation. "So you partnered with my brother to kill me, you shameless ingrate!" she began.

Fa'iza tried hopelessly to explain and justify her involvement. Munis remained unmoved. "So you always thought I was an idiot because I have a round face," she said.

"What? Who ever thought that?" Fa'iza responded vehemently.

"You! You bastard," returned Munis.

"I swear on the grave of the Holy Prophet I never thought that."

"Don't even try to fool me," Munis said with a steady stare. "I can read your mind now. Not only did you think I was stupid because of my round face, you also thought you could exploit my simplicity and work your way into marrying my brother. Isn't that so?"

"I swear to the spirits . . ."

"Oh, shut up! Stop swearing false oaths," Munis interrupted. Fa'iza went silent, eyes downcast.

"Now, look up at me," Munis said. "You will notice that my face is no longer round, but long."

Fa'iza looked up slowly. What she saw threw her into a fit of horror and mental disarray. In fact the woman's face had elongated and resembled that of a horse. She felt as if she was delirious, feverish. She wished she were paralyzed, blind, and deaf.

"Not only is my face long," Munis said petulantly, "so are the pupils of my eyes."

Shuddering with fear, Fa'iza looked into her eyes. Sure enough, the pupils had turned lozenge-shaped.

"Not only are they long, they are also red," said Munis.

As Munis spoke, Fa'iza saw a sinister red glow emanating from the woman's pupils. Impulsively, she looked down at Munis's feet, somehow expecting to see hooves.

"No, I don't have hooves," said Munis, laughing demonically.

Overcome with shock, Fa'iza was on the verge of passing out, but Munis was not about to let her. "Stop acting up!" she screamed.

"There is something unclean in your nature," Munis continued, "but I have decided to live with you and leave this house. I want to set up an organization, make an example of my brother, to prevent other brothers from killing their sisters. In reality, I am not an evil person. But remember, I know whatever thoughts go through that tiny brain of yours. Understand?"

"Of course, of course," Fa'iza breathed.

"My grandma, may God rest her soul," Munis went on, "had a cat that accidentally got caught in a bedroll for twenty four hours. When it was rescued, it was as thin and long as a book. It gorged itself with so much food that it swelled up and died. When I came out of the grave I had the same feeling as that cat. I have a feeling its spirit has transmigrated into me."

"Of course," Fa'iza said in agreement, "you are probative in your observation. Your eyes have feline contours and your face does tend to display equine features."

"What kind of weird, bookish talk is that?" Munis protested vehemently. "We were friends until a few weeks ago, although you did think I was stupid. But we were still friends. Talk normally."

"Very well," Fa'iza said obediently.

"Besides I have read the book on men and women," Munis said, "and you can't think you know more than I do. Get it?"

"Yes."

"Furthermore, I want you to know that Parveen is a better cook than you are. This is my considered opinion. Understand?"

This brought a lump to Fa'iza's throat, making her look flustered and broken-hearted. Munis, once of the round face, felt a tinge of pity.

"Of course your cooking is not bad," she said consolingly, "but hers is better."

"What are we going to do now?" asked Fa'iza, to change the subject.

"We'll just wait for the bride and groom to return," Munis answered.

Several hours later the wedding party, including the parents and a large number of close friends and relatives, arrived in an exuberant, festive mood, yipping and yodeling loudly in celebration. Ceremoniously they ushered the bride, who pretended reluctance, into the bridal chamber. The groom, drunk to the point of incapacity, was next.

Suddenly Alia gave a piercing scream and slumped to the floor. She had caught sight of Munis, who was standing to the side of the hall watching the crowd. Haji Sorkhchehreh also noticed her.

"Who would this lady be?" he asked of no one in particular.

"Munis! Oh, my daughter," the mother exclaimed, more in surprise than in answer to the question.

Munis did not say a word. She pushed her way through the crowd to the bridal chamber touching the door softly.

Although locked from inside, the door opened slowly to let her in, and closed behind her. Amir, barely able to stand, was in the process of undressing in a corner of the room. Looking embarrassed and shy, the young bride was doing the same in another corner. At the sound of the slamming door, they both turned to see Munis standing in the middle of the room. The bride was utterly confused at the sight of the stranger, but Amir was nearly shocked to death. Munis's face lengthened and her eyes narrowed to a slit.

"Stop playing," she told her brother. "Step forward like a man."

Amir advanced toward her involuntarily.

"You miserable wretch," she addressed him, "Why are you so drunk?"

"What can I say? I am."

"So you married an eighteen-year-old because she is pristine and chaste?"

"Yes."

"And you," Munis turned to the girl. "Didn't you get knocked up last year by your cousin? And didn't you have an abortion by Mrs. Fatemi?"

The young woman nearly lost her balance, but Munis caught her before she collapsed. "Enough of these theatrics," Munis told her. "It was at the suggestion of this very Mrs. Fatemi that you got my stupid brother drunk tonight, wasn't it?" Without waiting for an answer, she turned to Amir.

"And you, bastard," she hissed, "You must live and make do with her. If you raise your hand to her, or hurt her in any way, I will return and swallow you whole. Do you understand?" Amir nodded in the affirmative.

"I am going to live with Fa'iza," she told the couple standing in front of her motionless. "That poor woman, though a little full of herself, was at least a virgin, and this one isn't. This is what happens to stupid men. But as I said before, if you hurt her, I'll take it out on you in a way that you'll never forget as long as you live."

She then left the room and crossed the hall toward the living room. Alia, who had regained consciousness, followed her. So did her mother and the rest of the guests. Haji Sorkhchehreh wanted to know why the sister of the groom was not at the wedding. The mother was evasive, unable to talk to her daughter in front of the guests. Besides, she harbored a vague inner fear of her daughter.

"Sister," Munis addressed Fa'iza, who had stayed behind in the living room, " let's go to Karadj."

"Oh, please take me with you," Alia pleaded.

"Later, later," said Munis.

The crowd, dazed and quiet, parted as the two women made their way to the front door and disappeared in the dark of the night.

Mrs. Farrokhlaqa Sadroddin Golchehreh

FARROKHLAQA, FIFTY-ONE YEARS OLD, but as beautiful
and impeccably groomed as ever, lounged in an Ameri-
can-style rocking chair on the balcony. It was mid-spring
and the air was redolent with the scent of citrus blossoms.
She closed her eyes and concentrated on the fragrance.
She reminded herself that if her father had been alive, he
would be crouching at the corner of the yard tending to
his favorite geranium pots. He had died ten years earlier,
but it was as if he had just died the day before. "My dear
girl," he said two days before his death, "I have my reser-
vations about that man." He said that, and died two days
later.

For a moment the recollections of her father over-whelmed her focus on the fragrance, but she lifted her right hand to her face, as if to keep the memory from entering her mind. It was so melancholy to think of the dead.

Golchehreh was in the room. He was putting on his tie in front of a full-length mirror, which reflected part of the yard, and the balcony where his wife, deep in thought, was gently rocking in the chair. He was taking his time as he watched his wife's reflection in the mirror. He did not cherish face-to-face encounters with his wife. On those occasions Golchehreh could only grin contemptuously and feel an intense dislike for her in his heart. But in her absence, or as he now watched her reflection in the mir-ror, he felt an overwhelming tenderness for her and loved her more than anything or anybody, a far cry from the deep set, thirty-year-old resentment he felt when they were in close proximity to each other.

Farrokhlaqa felt like stretching as she sat in the chair. She extended her arms and arched her back. This gave her a pleasurable release, but more than that it reminded her of Vivien Leigh in *Gone with the Wind*. That was how she had stretched in a bedroom scene. Thinking of Vivien Leigh reminded her of her encounter with Fakhroddin Azod at the banquet given by the Prince* at his Shem-iran estate. He had just returned from America and had brought with him many interesting pictures and home

* The title "Prince" is often given informally to individuals who are either descendants or relatives of the former royal family, the Qajar dynasty.

movies he had shot in New York and showed them to guests at parties. Farrokhlaqa had visited New York three times but had never seen the city as depicted in Fakhroddin's pictures. Secretly, she blamed her husband. He would descend to the hotel lobby at nine, have breakfast, hang around the common areas and bars, go back to the room, take naps, and wait for their host, Mr. Entezam, to pick them up at night and take them to a restaurant, movie theater, or nightclub.

By now the husband had finished knotting his tie and was looking for some other excuse to prolong his stay in front of the mirror. He thought of giving himself a shave. That would afford him another half hour to stay at his vantage point. He went to the bathroom and returned with his shaving paraphernalia and a towel. He began the ritual slowly and with much deliberation, while his wife waited patiently for him to finish and leave the house. Since his retirement Golchehreh had taken up the habit of going for a walk every afternoon. For two hours he walked around the neighborhood, stopping at a local café to read the newspaper. His wife looked forward to his absence so she could move around freely. With him in the house, she felt restricted and claustrophobic—a need to confine herself to a corner to avoid contact. In the thirty-two years of their marriage she had learned to be inactive when her husband was home. Instinctively she felt vitality and joy in his absence. In the old days, with Golchehreh at work for at least eight hours a day—although he came home for lunch and a nap—she was more active and energetic. She had even taken voice lessons. Since his retirement, she had lost that dynamism. The man was not only always at home, he was also in the way. He did not show any interest in gardening or fixing the plaster molding of the reception hall ceiling, which was in a sorry state of disrepair. He was always in his pajamas, languishing in an armchair. Often he would tease Farrokhlaqa with his off-color jokes.

"You could shave in the bathroom," the wife suggested. "You'll get the carpet wet."

Golchehreh, as he dipped his brush in the water bowl, saw this as an opening for a snide remark. "Shut up, Your Ladyship!" he retorted.

Farrokhlaqa bit her lip, turning her head, unwilling to start a row, although the words burst into her head with an explosive force looking for an outlet, and it came when she thought of Fakhroddin Azod. She often took refuge in thinking of him in moments of distress.

That night, that meeting at a reception after his return from America, she was standing under a locust tree.

"Vivien Leigh!" he exclaimed, approaching her from behind.

She turned to look at him. She still remembered those sensuous lips. Although she had kissed them many times later, the memory of that sight of those well-shaped lips, pressed together, as if to hide the glint of his perfect white teeth, was always fresh in her mind.

"Are you talking to me?" she said, trying to sound surprised.

"Yes, you," he replied, "the delicate little sister of Vivien Leigh. The resemblance is astounding."

She wanted to turn her head and look at him from the corner of her eye, a posture she had learned from her mother, but she couldn't quite make it. Instead, she felt intimidated and nervous at the sight of Fakhroddin's fleshy lips now parted in a charming smile.

"Farrokh," he said, abbreviating her name as a gesture of familiarity, "Believe me, you are getting more beautiful day by day. It's unbelievable!"

By now she had gained enough composure to turn her head on her left shoulder and glance at the man from the corner of her eye.

"But you haven't seen me in ten years," she remarked.

"What do you mean I haven't?" he asked, his tone suggesting surprise. "How is it possible?"

"So where have you seen me?"

"Here," said Fakhroddin, as he beat his fist over his heart several times. "Why did you get married?"

"I shouldn't have?"

"Did you have to?"

Farrokhlaqa was perplexed. She had never promised him anything. She was only thirteen when he had left for America. She didn't remember having any feelings for him at the time.

"That's life," she said, with a shrug of her shoulders. "People get married."

"And you, too?" he said, with a grin. "A woman of exceptional beauty, you didn't have the right to marry. You should have given all the men in the world the opportunity to feast their eye."

The comment made her laugh. She was briefly concerned that he might be offended by her laughter. But he wasn't.

"Always wear blue," he said as he sidled up to her. "It becomes you so well."

Suddenly out of nowhere Golchehreh interjected himself between them. He did not even reach Fakhroddin's shoulder. He had his usual annoying grin and suspicious look, the source of constant distress for her in the four years of their marriage.

"I was telling your lady about the movie *Gone with the Wind*," said Fakhroddin. "It had just opened when I saw it before I left. You don't know the trouble I had to get a ticket. I had to get in line at five in the morning. I was telling her how very much she looks like Vivien Leigh, the star of the movie."

All Golchehreh could come up with was a hollow, "Oh, really," accompanied by his customary spiteful grin. He had sense enough to know that he compared unfavorably to Fakhroddin.

"Make sure you see it when it's playing here," advised Fakhroddin. "It is a great masterpiece of the movie industry, and the costliest so far."

They returned home that night in her uncle's car. Intimidated by the uncle's gravitas, Golchehreh remained silent during the trip. At the end of the alley, they got out and politely said goodbye to the old man and walked side-by-side toward the house. Farrokhlaqa thought that her husband would go to bed directly, leaving her alone to revel in the events of the evening. But that was not to be. From the moment they were dropped off, he kept up a litany of sarcastic comments about "that bloke," his lousy taste in movies, his stupid photographs, and that ridiculous American-Indian feathered warbonnet he had brought with him from America that all the guests, including Farrokhlaqa, wanted to have their picture taken in. She was only able to say, "Oh, shut up," in a voice muffled by a lump in her throat.

The only effect of this utterance was for Golchehreh to shift the focus of his acrimony to her, beginning with the blue dress that according to him looked so ugly and tasteless that it made everybody sick. At two in the morning, he brought a watermelon from the cellar and started eating it, insisting that she should have some as well. She put up with the nuisance, hoping to have a little time before sleep to savor the encounter with Fakhroddin.

Then, after the watermelon, Golchehreh turned on the radio, tuning in broadcasts in Persian from Berlin, London, or Moscow so he could catch up with the affairs of the world. Finally, around three in the morning he climbed into bed demanding that she fulfill what he referred to as her marital obligations. She submitted mechanically to his unwanted attention. By now it was four in the morning. He declared his intention to take a shower in preparation for performing the morning prayers, something he did only occasionally.

From that night on, Farrokhlaqa felt a deep-seated, permanent loathing for her husband.

HAVING NOW FINISHED SHAVING, Golchehreh began to slowly gather his things to take them to the bathroom.

He did not know why he was so sluggish that day, as if he was trying to delay something untoward from happening, but he wasn't sure what.

The doorbell rang. Mosayeb the manservant rushed to answer it. Impatiently, Farrokhlaqa waited to see who was calling. Her husband had moved onto the balcony and stood a short distance behind her chair. They exchanged glances reflecting their mutual distaste for each other.

"You'll be fifty-one next month," said Golchehreh casually, as if expressing a random thought. "You'll be menopausal, Fakhur Dear."

She stared at him for a long moment, knowing that he was intent on tormenting her.

"Listen to me, Sadri," she said venomously, "if you think you can joke around with me, think again."

"I'm not joking," he protested mockingly, "menopause is no joke."

Mosayeb returned from the door with the newspaper and put it on the floor at her feet. Before he left he said something about going to the butcher shop in Karadj to get meat for Friday night's party.

"I wish we had an orchard in Karadj," she said as she picked up the newspaper and glanced at the front page.

"Do you think you will have the energy in menopause to mess around with an orchard?" her husband asked with a chuckle.

"Do you think you want to have a baby at your age?" she retorted contemptuously. "Isn't that why you bring up the issue of menopause?"

"Perhaps I do want to have a baby at my age," he replied. "Not that it is possible with Your Ladyship anymore."

"Very well, then," she fumed, "you can get yourself a servant girl. You've always had that lowly disposition."

She then returned to the paper, ignoring him. Golchehreh reached out and grabbed the paper, which she relinquished without resistance, returning her gaze to the garden below. Mosayeb, now ready to go for his shopping chores, shouted from garden, "Do you want anything else?"

"If you find fresh almonds, get some," she answered. Mosayeb left without a word.

Golchehreh, perched on the narrow ledge of a window, was looking through the paper. Why doesn't he go for his walk, Farrokhlaqa wondered. She desperately wanted to resume her reminiscing. She remembered the day they had gone to pay a courtesy visit to Fakhroddin's American wife, who had just joined her husband six months after his return, with their two sons, Teddy and Jimmy. How strange those names sounded to her at the time. She remembered how nervous she had been all day. She had curled her hair and carefully selected a white dress with blue flowers. Her husband, with his habitual derisive grin, watched her as she put on her makeup and fixed her hair. She even spent time making sure that the seams of her nylons were perfectly straight. She was satisfied with what she saw when she gave herself a last look in the hall mirror.

She had never seen an American woman, but she had

made a point of going to see *Gone with the Wind*. Compared to Vivien Leigh, she did not find herself lacking, although she didn't think she resembled her. But there must be some likeness, she had decided, if Fakhroddin says so.

The Azods were staying with relatives while their residence, on the northern side of the family estate, was being made ready for them. The American woman was standing at the wide entrance to the reception hall shaking hands with arriving guests. She did not know Persian and did not speak but acknowledged each visitor with a smile. She was tall and had blond hair. Her hands were marked with veins and freckles. Her eyes were light blue, so light they were almost colorless with only the slightest hint of blue. Well, Fakhroddin was partial to blue. Farrokhlaqa shook hands with the woman and passed along the wall where there was a mirror. She stared at her own dark eyes and the blue floral pattern of her dress in the mirror. She then caught a fleeting glimpse of Fakhroddin's reflection as he passed behind her.

Why did you get married? She mentally addressed the question to his reflection, in the same spirit that she herself had been asked the question not long ago. In her imagination Farrokhlaqa saw him as pale, and mouthing the words "Always wear white with blue flowers. It becomes you so well." He hastened to join his wife at the reception line. But they kept running into each other, as if a force brought them together throughout the course of the evening.

Years later, on the terrace of the Prince's villa, Farrokhlaqa had told Adeleh Raf'at about the affair. Adeleh was a good woman. She had made an effort to understand the situation and had sympathized with Farrokhlaqa for giving in to love, criticizing Golchehreh for his odious conduct. There was a rumor going around among their acquaintances about a liaison between Adeleh and the Prince. Farrokhlaqa had structured her own narrative in such a way as to make it easier for Adeleh to open up and talk about her affair with the Prince. Her strategy worked. Adeleh tearfully confided in her and the bond between them grew strong.

"It went on for eight years," Farrokhlaqa told her about her own affair, "eight strange years."

"So you were a lover throughout the war years," Adeleh observed. "Good for you, girl."

Now, on the balcony, Farrokhlaqa clasped her hands behind her head and stretched as she yawned. "Eight years of war," she said loudly.

Golchehreh felt increasingly irritable without knowing why. He suddenly asked, "In menopause, do women undergo an emotional shift as well?"

"I don't know."

"It must be so," he speculated. "That is why polygamy is allowed for a man so he won't have to put up with a menopausal woman in his bed for the rest of his life."

"Perhaps," said Farrokhlaqa.

Golchehreh was reminded of that Polish émigré woman he had met in a tavern during the war. The woman knew little Persian and Golchehreh had taken to calling her Farrokhlaqa. She had a hard time pronouncing it and thought it sounded funny.

"Faroklaka return Europa," she had mumbled, laughing heartily, on the day that the news of the end of the war had reached Tehran. She was gone the following week.

"Will you be very upset if I marry another woman?" Golchehreh asked musingly. There was no reaction from Farrokhlaqa, who was gazing at the garden, deep in thought. She was thinking of the last time she had looked into Fakhroddin's face.

They were in his house, the door locked and curtains drawn. In the darkness of the room his eyes gleamed strangely.

"I need to go," he had said. "I need to go and take care of my children."

Farrokhlaqa was weeping soundlessly. "But I will return," he said resolutely. "I promise I will."

When the war ended, the American wife returned with Teddy and Jimmy. She acted erratically and seemed emotionally perturbed. At a party one night she had stood up and yelled, "You are all crazy." It could have been the alcohol, or that the stress had been too much for her. Ten days later she took her children and left for America.

For some reason, Farrokhlaqa knew deep down in her heart that Fakhroddin would never come back to her. Five months later came the news that he had died in a car crash. She felt she was now alone in the world with only Golchehreh for company. Of course there were the children, but they had their own lives. They had grown so fast it was as if they had never been born.

Golchehreh had finished with the paper. He folded it and held it ready in anticipation of his wife wanting it back. This would open a line of conversation for him to talk about menopause, further annoying his wife. He had seen the word and learned about it in a reference book only three days earlier. He could foresee that a discussion of it would irritate her.

Farrokhlaqa persisted in her awkward silence. Her husband grew impatient and asked, "Don't you want the paper?" She reached out wordlessly and took it out of his hand. She then lit a cigarette.

"You mustn't smoke," her husband warned. "At your age and with menopause coming you'll seriously hurt yourself."

"Why don't you go for a walk?" she said, more as a suggestion than a question. "You go every day."

"Perhaps I don't feel like it today," he answered sharply.

She regretted asking the question. She was certain he would never leave the house if he suspected that his absence was a relief to her in any way.

"That's fine," she said, sounding nonchalant. "It is better if you stay home today."

"On second thought," he said, rising to his feet, "I think I'll go for stroll after all."

He felt hesitant to leave, as if something was likely to happen in his absence. He stood in front of her, thinking for a moment that it was no longer necessary to wear that sarcastic grin when looking at her. He realized that the grin was his defensive barrier against her overwhelming desirability. Suddenly he did not feel the need for this barrier. He had an urge to look at her the way he looked at the Polish woman in the bar, the one he gave the name Farrokhlaqa. It was true his wife was now on the verge of menopause. She did not dream anymore, and went to bed early. She even snored sometimes. Perhaps he could now look at her in a natural, spontaneous way.

He followed her as she left the room, intercepting her at the landing. He interposed himself between her and the staircase with his back to the stairs.

"Farrokhlaqa darling," he said.

There was a tremor of surprise in the woman. He had never addressed her in those terms. He always called her by a nickname. And that loathsome grin was not there. Instead there was in the tone of his voice a trace of what sounded like genuine affection. She shuddered with fear. She was certain there was an evil intention behind all this. "What if he wants to kill me?" she thought to herself. Instinctively, she sank her fist in his midriff as hard as she could. Under the blow his belly felt soft and resistless. It threw him off-balance. He tried uselessly to keep his foothold on the stairs but he could not. He took a head-long fall down the staircase. Farroklaqa steadied herself by leaning on a chair nearby. She averted her eyes from the bottom of the staircase where the man was sprawled on the floor, motionless.

Three months later, shriveled and dressed in black, Farrokhlaqa was sitting on a chair. Mosayeb was delivering a message from Mr. Ostovary, the real-estate agent. In case the lady thought of selling the house, she should let him know. At one point she had casually told Mosayeb that she might want to sell the house if Ostovary could find her a suitable garden villa in Karadj. Ostovary had found one near the river.

Mrs. Farrokhlaqa Sadroddin Golchehreh bought the villa, sold the house, and moved to Karadj.

Zarrinkolah

ZARRINKOLAH WAS TWENTY-SIX and a prostitute. She lived at Golden Akram's brothel in the city's notorious red-light district. Akram, the madam, had seven gold teeth. That was why some people called her "Akram the Seven."

Zarrinkolah had lived there since puberty. In the early years she had three or four customers a day, but now at twenty-six, she serviced twenty, twenty-five, even thirty customers a day. Several times she had complained to Akram about the pressure of work, but all she got was a tongue lashing, and once even a beating. She had learned her lesson.

Zarrinkolah was a jolly person by nature. She had always been cheerful—from the time when she received three or four guests a day until now when she handled twenty or thirty. She even expressed her complaints as jokes. The women liked her tremendously. During lunch breaks she would crack jokes or carry out comedy routines, and the women responded with peals of laughter.

On some occasions she toyed with the idea of leaving the house, but the women had pleaded with her to stay. Without her, they said, the house would be cheerless. It was possible that some of them had egged Akram on to beat her. In reality, she was never serious about leaving; she had no place else to go but to another establishment like this one. At nineteen she had had a real chance of leaving when she had a suitor. He was an ambitious bricklayer who dreamed of becoming a contractor. Unfortunately, before he could carry through with his proposal, he had his skull split by a shovel in a fight. By now Zarrinkolah was resigned to her fate, although she complained from time to time.

But for the past six months Zarrinkolah had been experiencing a serious problem with the way her mind worked. It all started one Saturday morning. She got up, drank a glass of water, and was getting ready for breakfast. "Zarry," she heard Akram shout from downstairs. "You have a customer and he is in a hurry."

Usually, there were no customers in the morning, except those who had stayed overnight and fancied extra treatment before they left. So what? Zarrinkolah had thought to herself that morning, to hell with customers so early in the morning.

Before she could give voice to her thoughts, she heard Akram's voice again, louder and sharper this time, "I'm talking to you, Zarry. The customer is on his way."

Zarrinkolah gave up on breakfast. Angrily she went back to her room, threw herself on the bed and parted her thighs.

The customer came into the room. It was a man with no head. She was so frightened she couldn't scream. She submitted to him frozen with fear. He finished his business and left. That day all her customers were headless. She kept it to herself afraid that she might be accused of being possessed by evil spirits. She had heard of another woman afflicted with evil possession who would let out blood-curdling screams around eight o'clock at night scaring away customers at the peak of business hours. The woman had been turned out of the house and had disappeared without a trace. Zarrinkolah had assumed that the time the spirits visited was eight at night. She thought of singing at that hour to ward them off. For the past six months she had been breaking into song at eight o'clock. Unfortunately she had a poor voice and could not carry a tune. "You slut," a traveling musician, frustrated by her singing off key, had barked at her. "You have no voice and you've given me a headache." After that Zarrinkolah had taken to going down to the basement washroom to practice out of earshot. Akram the Seven was watching her bizarre routine, but didn't mind it as long as she served her daily quota of customers and did so cheerfully.

After a while, a fifteen-year-old girl was recruited to join the house. She was painfully shy. One day Zarrinkolah beckoned her upstairs to her room.

"Listen to me, kid," she addressed her, "I have to tell you something. I have to tell someone, or I'll go mad. It is a secret that's eating me up."

"Of course one has to confide in someone," said the girl, sounding precocious. "My grandma told me that when His Holiness Ali* couldn't find anyone to trust with his thoughts, he would go into the desert, lean into an abandoned well, and tell his secrets."

"That's right," said Zarrinkolah, "now I'm telling you that I see all people without heads, I mean men, not women.

"Do you really?" said the girl sympathetically, without any trace of skepticism.

"Yes!"

"Perhaps they really don't have any heads."

"But other women would notice something like that, too."

"That is true," the girl said contemplatively. "It is possible they also see the men headless but like you are afraid to talk about it."

So they agreed to exchange signals if either one of them saw a headless man. The experiment indicated that only Zarrinkolah saw headless men.

---

* Ali-ibn-Abitalib, Prophet Mohammed's nephew and the first imam in the Twelve Shiite tradition, highly venerated in Iran.

"Zarrinkolah," the girl addressed her with an air of authority, "You must say your prayers. You should give alms. Perhaps you will be able to see men with heads again."

Zarrinkolah asked Akram the Seven for a two-day furlough. She headed to the local bathhouse, and reserved a private stall for herself. She also asked for a masseuse and told the woman to scrub every inch of her body with utmost care. She ordered the masseuse to repeat the process three times. By now Zarrinkolah's skin was raw with excessive scrubbing as if blood was about to seep out of her pores. The masseuse was exhausted and almost on the verge of tears. "You poor woman," she said, "You're insane."

Zarrinkolah gave her a hefty tip and asked for her discretion. She then asked the masseuse to teach her the process of devotional ablution. After the masseuse left, she performed the ablution ritual meticulously, and kept repeating it over and over, nearly fifty times, still feeling her skin on fire from the severity of the scrubbing the masseuse had given her.

Finally she decided to get dressed and prepare for a visit to the shrine of Shah Abdolazim. But she felt an urge to prostrate herself, naked as she was, in prayer and plead for God's grace. It occurred to her that she did not remember the required formalities and incantations for such an appeal. She then remembered Imam Ali and his agony in telling his secrets to a well. She thought of invoking his name and asking for his intercession with God on her behalf.

"Ali, Ali, Ali," she moaned repeatedly as she dropped to her knees naked and pressed her forehead on the floor. She then burst into a fit of sobbing, still repeating "Ali, Ali, Ali."

Someone was beating on the door of the stall.

"Who is it?" she asked, still crying.

"We're closing the bathhouse for the night," came the answer.

Zarrinkolah put on fresh clothes, leaving the old ones behind, and started walking toward the shrine. By the time she got there the shrine was closed for the night. She sat on the grass near the gate. The sky was cloudless, and the courtyard was lit up by moonlight. Zarrinkolah wept soundlessly.

When the gate to the shrine was opened in the morning, Zarrinkolah's eyes were no more than narrow slits in her face, her eyes having receded behind swollen eyelids. She did not enter the shrine. She was not crying anymore. She felt as light as air, like a piece of straw being carried along by the wind. From a street vendor she bought a bowl of porridge.

"Where can one find a breath of cool air in this beastly summer heat?" she asked the vendor.

"Karadj isn't bad," he replied, looking at her swollen eyes compassionately.

She headed for Karadj.

Two Women on the Road

AT SUNSET TWO WOMEN, one twenty-eight and the other thirty-eight years old, both wearing chadors, were walking along the highway to Karadj. They were both virgins.

At mile marker eighteen, a truck came to a halt thirty feet away from them. There were three men in the cab. The driver and his assistant were drunk; the passenger was not. Several times along the trip, the passenger had had to grab the steering wheel to avoid a collision, or to stop the truck from running off the road. Finally, he had given up on interfering and decided to let fate take its course.

When the truck stopped, the driver beckoned to his assistant to get out. The two walked toward the women.

The passenger took the opportunity to stretch and light a cigarette.

"Where are you ladies heading?" asked the driver when he reached the women.

The twenty-eight-year-old, Fa'iza, promptly came up with the answer, "We are going to Karadj to live by the fruits of our own labor and not to have any men to order us around."

"Is that so?" said the driver. "Are you serious?" He suddenly reached for her chador and pulled it off her head.

"What the hell," she yelled with a mixture of fear and surprise. "Help! Help!"

At once the men attacked the women and a struggle ensued. The woman named Fa'iza continued to resist and scream as she was forced to the ground. The other, named Munis, quit fighting and remained inert.

After fifteen minutes the men got to their feet and started to dust themselves off slowly, without any fear of being caught in the act. The two women remained on the ground, with Fa'iza cursing the aggressors. "I hope God will take our revenge," she said defiantly as the men tidied themselves up.

"The one I ended up with was not that hot," said the assistant with some dissatisfaction.

"That was your lot, boy," said the driver grinning. "Mine on the other hand put up a delicious fight, pretending she was chaste." They both chuckled at the remark.

Mockingly, the men thanked the women and moved toward their truck. The driver started the engine.

"Did something happen back there?" asked the passenger.

"None of your business," barked the driver.

"Sorry," the passenger responded apologetically, "I thought there was an accident or something."

"What is it to you, anyway? Are you a policeman?"

"No, I'm a gardener. They call me 'Kind Gardener.'"

"Hey, Kind Gardener," the driver said, amused, "we were irrigating the fields."

The driver and his assistant were hugely amused by the comment. They broke out into laughter. The driver was laughing so hard that he lost control of the steering wheel and the truck began to swerve wildly on the highway. To avoid a head-on collision with a Mercedes sedan, he jerked the wheel, which sent the truck off the road toward a clump of trees. The truck smashed the first tree but came to shattering halt against the next. The door on the passenger side blew open sucking out the assistant and threw him on the ground just as the truck capsized over him. The impact sent the driver flying through the windshield toward power lines directly overhead. He was followed by the passenger, who crashed into a large pile of mud on the side of the road.

The driver, who had instinctively grabbed at a high-voltage cable to stop his flight, was electrocuted. His body convulsed not unlike some macabre dance movements. The assistant had been crushed to death instantly, before he had a chance to open his eyes.

The passenger rose to his feet slowly, trying to extricate himself from the mud pile. He surveyed the scene of death and destruction around him.

"Oh, villainous creatures!" he exclaimed.

Soon he realized he could not wipe the muddy substance off of him without a shower and change of clothes. He found his right shoe, put it on, and started ambling in the direction of Karadj.

Farrokhlaqa's Garden

Part One

FARROKHLAQA WAS SPRAWLED in the back seat of the car. Ostovary, Mosayeb, and the driver were in the front. That is how they arrived at the gate of the garden at four in the afternoon. Ostovary was worried about his client's reaction to the tree. Except for that, he had discussed all aspects of the property with her. As soon as the car came to a halt, he jumped out ahead of the driver and opened the car door for her. It was the driver's last day of work. In fact he didn't even have to work that day. The lady could have driven herself. But he had offered to drive ostensibly as a favor, but more to satisfy his own curiosity about the property she was about to acquire.

"You will notice what a jewel this property is," Ostovary said.

Ignoring his pitch, Farrokhlaqa walked toward the gate ahead of the men. She stopped in front of the gate, turned her head to the left shoulder, a pose she had learned from her mother, and asked, "Is that it?"

"Yes, ma'am," Ostovary answered, producing a large key from his pocket. "Allow me," he said as he opened the gate and stepped back for the woman to pass.

Cautiously, Farrokhlaqa stepped across the threshold, trembling with excitement, which she tried to hide from her companions. Nonchalantly she started to walk along the gravel path while voraciously taking in every detail.

"Exactly as you desired, madam," Ostovary noted, "just a few minor touchups here and there, and it will look gorgeous." Farrokhlaqa nodded her head, acknowledging the remark.

The path circled around a reflecting pool with a bedstead next to it and led to the mosaic steps in front of the house. The building did not look very attractive. It was a slapdash, contractor-built job and it showed. Farrokhlaqa felt a tinge of disappointment.

"A coat of stucco would do the façade wonders," Ostovary suggested.

Farrokhlaqa considered it for a moment. It wasn't a bad idea, she thought. In fact it was a good idea, she decided, as she looked at the windows and found them of proper size, given the local climate.

Ostovary unlocked the front door to a spacious, cool entrance hall, with three large rooms on each side as well as a kitchen, a shower room, and a bathroom. The windows of the rooms looked out onto the garden and a narrow backyard.

"I like the kitchen," was Farrokhlaqa's first comment. "It is nice and big. But just one shower is not enough. We also need more than three rooms. I expect a lot of company."

"As I said earlier, madam," Ostovary said, "The foundation is firm and steel beams have been used in the framework. You can add another floor with no problem." As he moved to another corner of the hall he added expansively, "A staircase could go from here to the top floor. An atrium could be set up here with a tree growing through to the next floor, even through the roof. It will look palatial."

The thought of a tree growing inside a house befuddled Farrokhlaqa. "I came up with that idea myself," Ostovary said with a touch of pride.

"We'll see about that," Farrokhlaqa declared, unconvinced. "As the tree grows, it will damage the foundation." She had liked the house, although she knew she should not display enthusiasm in front of Ostovary. She had already decided on adding a second floor and fancied an expanded, dynamic social life with friends coming to visit on weekends and holidays. Thirty-two years of living with a cranky, temperamental man had lost her many friends. But that might be a blessing: she could initiate new friendships and associations of her own choice, with artists, writers, scholars, turning her parlor into a salon, in the fashion of high-class ladies of eighteenth-century Paris she had read about in novels. In the meantime, Ostovary kept up a running commentary as they continued the inspection of various parts of the property. He even counted the trees and had ideas about each. To keep up the garden, it would be necessary to hire a horticulturist, he believed. The garden had been left untended for a year and looked wild and overgrown.

Ostovary had arranged for the tour to be punctuated with stops at various trees, about each of which he had comments or ideas. "Madam," he said, "you will not find a better deal in all of Karadj. To be honest, there are nicer homes and gardens here, but for the price you are paying, this is the very best. With minor improvements, this will turn into a paradise." Farrokhlaqa had already made up her mind to buy the property and considered Ostovary's solicitations redundant, but she let him go through his routine.

By now they had reached the river. "As you notice," said Ostovary somewhat pompously. "The riverbank is the property line. The water current is so fast here that there is no danger of burglars crossing it. Besides, there are no burglars among the people here."

"Is that so?" said Farrokhlaqa absent-mindedly, as her attention was drawn to the tree, finding it hard to believe that it was real. "Who is that?" she asked in amazement. Ostovary, who had anticipated this moment with dread, tried to answer as casually as possible: "Actually . . . this is a human being. But I promise you," he continued, trying to reassure his client, "she is the most harmless person you'll ever meet in your life."

"So? What is she doing here?"

"How shall I say?" Ostovary stammered. "They let the property go so cheap because of this particular detail. I thought it would be a pity for you not to take advantage of the situation, especially, being a woman yourself, you could definitely tolerate this poor tree."

Apprehensively, Farrokhlaqa stepped closer. "But this is not a tree; it's a person."

"That is quite so," affirmed Ostovary. "Actually this poor tree . . . is the sister of the former owner of the property," he added, as if mortified by the irrationality of his own statement.

"How strange!" Farrokhlaqa uttered sharply.

"It certainly is. This poor soul went mad and planted herself in the ground."

"But this is not going to work. She needs to be taken to the insane asylum."

"That is the problem," Ostovary explained. "This wretched woman disappeared in the autumn of last year. They searched everywhere for her and did not find her. Finally they gave up and when they came to the garden for the summer season, they found her planted here in the ground. Well, they realized she'd gone mad. I tell you, madam, they tried so hard to pull her out of the ground, but found it impossible."

Ostovary brought out a large bandana handkerchief from his pocket and dabbed his eyes. He then blew his nose in it noisily. Farrokhlaqa was somewhat moved by his emotional reaction to the narrative. "Is she not one of your own relatives, God forbid?" she asked.

"No way, I swear to God," he said vehemently. He

continued, "I haven't cried in twenty years, but every time I see this poor woman I cannot hold back my tears. Anyway, no matter how hard they tried, they couldn't get her out of the ground. And she pleaded with them 'Please, don't cut me down. Let me grow.'"

"But she hasn't sprouted any branches," Farrokhlaqa observed.

"No, not yet," he said, "although she has spread roots and perhaps she'll grow leaves by next year."

"What about her family?" she wanted to know.

"What shall I say?" he replied. "They are all upset and miserable because of this embarrassment. How can they tell people that their daughter or sister has turned into a tree? You can't tell people that. Any way, they came to see me and to consult with me. They said they'd let the property go cheap provided that the sellers remain anonymous. That is why you are able to buy the garden at a price well below the market value. It was your luck."

"Why were they embarrassed by her?" asked Farrokhlaqa, unwilling to leave the subject. "There is no shame in becoming a tree."

"What do you mean by that, madam?" Ostovary exclaimed with unaccustomed sharpness. "A sane person does not turn into a tree. One must be insane like this poor soul for the transformation to take place. The poor brother was crying when he told me, 'Soon people will find out about my sister becoming a tree and start making fun of us, for example, calling us the Arbormans, Arborsons, and so on, or cover our walls with graffiti, and ruin the century-old reputation of our family.'

"And I tell you, madam, these people are a reputable family. How could they admit that one of them has turned into a tree? It is different if some one in the family becomes a minister or a member of the parliament. In fact one could boast of a relative in those positions. But how could you tell people that a family member has become a tree? Her brother told me that they wouldn't have minded if she had become a milk maid, a dairy girl. After all, making yogurt is a trade. But becoming a tree? I don't know about that."

Farrokhlaqa moved around the tree, examining it carefully. Mosayeb and the driver were keeping their distance, afraid to come closer.

The tree appeared to be a woman in her late twenties. She was buried in the ground up to her knees, wearing a tattered dress, standing erect, watching her surroundings. Farrokhlaqa began to feel an attachment to the tree.

"I told her brother not to worry," Ostovary continued, "I told him I had found a respectable lady from a substantial family as a buyer. I told him she is a real lady. She will tolerate poor Mahdokht on her property and keep your secret. She understands the importance of reputation."

Farrokhlaqa was no longer listening to Ostovary. There was a sudden, radical shift in her mind. She was thinking of all she could do with this extraordinary tree. Not only could she build an entire literary movement around her, but she could also elevate herself to leadership positions in the political arena. There was no one else in the world who actually possessed such a phenomenon, which for the lack of a better term, she called human-tree. "Just as I was telling you, madam," Ostovary interrupted her thoughts, "you can have a tree in the house. You can put a wall around this one to avoid notoriety and unwanted attention."

With a human-tree in her possession, Farrokhlaqa thought, ignoring Ostovary, she would not need any other kind of tree. The fact that she had come to own it, meant that she was superior to others in native intelligence, intellectual capacity, spiritual and physical fitness. Others did not deserve to possess a human-tree because they did not have the capacity to understand the significance of the "human-tree." Not that she herself fully understood the existential implications of owning a human-tree, but intuitively she knew that the tree would bring her fame and fortune. "No, Mr. Ostovary," she responded to his interjection. "No need for a tree in the house. This one will remain here as is. I have no objection to it."

Ostovary heaved a visible sigh of relief. "I was afraid you might find this unacceptable," he admitted. "I was half thinking of buying the property myself, if you rejected the deal; only that I have six children and I was sure they would uproot the poor tree. Thank God you will go through with it."

Farrokhlaqa started walking toward the garden gate as she continued her reflections, oblivious to Ostovary's running commentary.

"Mosayeb, Akbar," she shouted at the men, "Go back to the city and bring me back my luggage."

"Are you going to stay here as of tonight?" Mosayeb asked. "The house is empty and unfurnished."

"It's not a problem," she replied, "I want to stay here and personally oversee the renovations." Turning to Ostovary, she asked if it were possible to find bricklayers and masons to start the work the next day.

Flabbergasted, Ostovary asked, "What is the hurry, madam? Stay in town for the time being. I will supervise the project. And Mosayeb will be here to help."

"No," Farrokhlaqa said emphatically. "I'll be here myself. I don't want it to take longer than a month."

There was a knock at the garden gate. "It will not be proper, madam," opined Mosayeb, as he moved toward the gate. "The local peasants don't know you and they are nosy. You see? They are already at the door."

"It's not a big deal," Farrokhlaqa said, "I'll teach them not to mess around with me."

Mosayeb opened the door to a man and woman. "Pardon me, young man," the man addressed Mosayeb. "Is there need for a gardener at this villa?"

"For sure, my man, for sure," Farrokhlaqa intervened, before Mosayeb could make a response. "Are you a gardener?"

"My dear lady," answered the man, "I am a gardener. They call me 'Kind Gardener.' I am well-known for having a green thumb. I touch a bush and it sprouts a hundred stems, and I grow a hundred blooms on each stem."

Farrokhlaqa's head was spinning, what with the human-tree and now the green-thumb gardener."

"Can you do construction work?" she asked.

"I can do everything, madam," he replied boastfully. "Everything."

"Who is that?" Farrokhlaqa asked, pointing to the woman beside him. "Your wife?"

"No, madam," he answered. "I met this poor woman on the Karadj highway, confused, not knowing where she was. When she saw me she screamed and threw herself at my feet, crying. I asked her why she cried and kissed my feet. She said I was the first man she'd seen in six months that had a head."

"Is she crazy?" Farrokhlaqa asked.

"I don't think so," said the man. "Anyway, she followed me here. She says her name is Zarrinkolah. She says at one time she did some sinful things, but she's now foresworn it all."

"Zarrinkolah," Farrokhlaqa addressed the woman. "Can you cook?"

"No, Ma'am," she answered.

"Can you do house cleaning?"

"No, Ma'am."

"How about washing dishes?"

"No, Ma'am."

"Then what can you do?"

"Madam," said the woman, "I can learn to do all these things. What I can do is tell stories and sing songs. Besides, although I am young, I have a world of experience."

"What is your real name?" Farrokhlaqa asked, turning to the gardener.

"What is the point of knowing my real name?" he answered. "Everyone calls me 'Kind Gardener.' You too can call me that."

"Gardener," she said, "as of today you are my employee. But what do we do about this woman?"

"Employ her, too," Kind Gardener suggested. "She'll mill around the place and learn to do things."

"So be it," said Farrokhlaqa. She thought the woman had the potential of becoming a useful addition to the house. She didn't look dishonest; in fact she appeared simple and sincere. Turning to the driver she ordered, "Bring back as much of the furniture and luggage as possible. Suitcases are packed and carpets are rolled. If necessary, rent a truck. I want everything here tonight."

She then ordered Ostovary to take Mosayeb with him to the town center and buy all the building material necessary for the renovation.

"But madam," Ostovary objected, "it is past six in the evening and everything is closed."

"Don't change the subject," she told him. "After all, we share a secret and we must help each other." Ostovary complied with her orders and left with Mosayeb.

"You just stay here close to me," she told Zarrinkolah.

"By all means, madam," she replied.

A couple of minutes after the men had left there was a knock on the garden gate. Farrokhlaqa opened the gate to find two women in soiled chadors, looking very exhausted and disheveled.

"What do you want?" asked Farrokhlaqa.

One of the pair burst out crying. The other, who looked older, waited for her companion to get over her emotional outburst.

"I am asking you," said Farrokhlaqa impatiently, "What do you want?"

"First of all, greetings, dear madam," the older woman began to speak. "My name is Munis and this is my friend Fa'iza. We have come a long way from Tehran and are very tired. And we have had some dreadful experiences along the way. If you permit us to stay here tonight, we will get back on the road tomorrow and follow our fate."

"Ladies," Farrokhlaqa said, "I am myself a new arrival here. I have no furniture. But I find it strange that two ladies like you should find yourselves stranded in this wilderness. You look like you are from respectable families. Why are you traveling unaccompanied?"

"It is a long story," Munis said. "The fact is that we decided to break out of the bondage of familial conventions and travel, to go on pilgrimages, explore the world. Unfortunately the first place we chose was Karadj, and a catastrophe happened."

Farrokhlaqa was intrigued. "Please, come in," she offered. "I expect some furniture tonight. Come on in and tell me what happened."

The new arrivals stepped into the garden and the group settled on the bedstead by the pool.

"Young lady," Farrokhlaqa addressed Fa'iza, who was still sobbing, "stop crying. It's not good for your health."

"On the contrary," interrupted Zarrinkolah. "Believe me, madam, I cried for twelve hours yesterday. This is not how my eyes look normally; they are big and brown. They are swollen because I cried so much. But that made me feel much better. Let her cry."

Farrokhlaqa patiently tolerated Zarrinkolah's interjection, but turned to Fa'iza again. "Now, miss, tell us what happened. Say something" she demanded.

Fa'iza was still crying, unable to speak.

"Dear madam," Munis added, "let me tell you that I had gotten it into my head to travel to India and the Orient in order to learn things for myself and not be told by others what to believe and what not to believe. I did not want to waste my life ignorant of transcendental truth. Of course, they say, ignorance is bliss, but I had decided to walk the path of enlightenment even if it meant suffering hardships. Naturally, when you embark on a journey you run risks. You either have the substance to overcome hardships or not. If you don't, you return to the flock like a poor little lamb. Even so, because you have taken the risk of stepping out, others think of you as mangy. You're avoided, ostracized. Again, you can either tolerate the situation or you can't, and you go kill yourself."

Munis stopped briefly and looked over her fascinated audience. "There is a lot to be said along these lines," she continued. "It so happened that this old friend became my traveling companion. I was afraid to leave her behind because she was likely to hurt herself—or hurt some other poor bastard more helpless than herself. I don't know why I thought the only exit out of Tehran was through Karadj. Can you imagine that? Now I realize there are other ways out of Tehran. You can leave through the airport, Shahr Rey, Niavaran, etc. But I only thought of Karadj. We were walking along the road when a truck pulled over. The drivers got out and raped us.

"Of course in all of this I see a mystery. I feel there was a force that wanted to confront me with a sample of the troubles I was to face in my journey. My poor friend here had the bad luck to be in my company. I now think with this bitter experience, I have taken the first step to discover a new jurisdiction, a new set of laws. As we were walking along I was thinking about how many people had to drown so that the first human could learn to swim. Even so, there are still those who drown. In any case, these thoughts are no consolation for my poor friend here."

Fa'iza managed to bring her sobbing under control enough to cut into Munis's monologue. "Madam," she addressed Farrokhlaqa, "but I was a virgin. At some point I want to get married. How can I deal with the dishonor of losing my virginity? How can I live down the disgrace?"

"But, my dear girl," said Munis, "I was a virgin, too. To hell with it. So what if we are not virgins anymore? Who cares?"

"But you are thirty-eight years old," returned Fa'iza. "Virginity is of no use to you anymore. I am only twenty-eight and still have a chance for a husband."

Farrokhlaqa was shocked. She thought the woman was very rude and insensitive to bring up her friend's age in that way. However, before she could make any comment, Munis turned to her and said, "No, Madam Farrokhlaqa, she is not rude. She knows I read minds. It is that simple. I know what goes on in her mind. So she's learned to be frank with me."

"Besides," Fa'iza continued, "you can change the shape

of your face and the pupils of your eyes. Why didn't you punish them for what they did to us?"

"Sweetheart," Munis said, "I can only read minds. Besides, I did want to punish them. But I didn't have to; they brought disaster upon themselves."

"How?" asked Farrokhlaqa.

"A couple of miles down the road they had a wreck. I didn't have to lift a finger."

"That's not true," Fa'iza objected. "We saw no wrecks on the road."

"My dear," said Munis, "we took a detour through the hills to avoid running into more rapists. But I know the truck crashed."

"How do you know?" asked Farrokhlaqa, her curiosity piqued.

"I just know. I read minds."

"Can you really read minds?"

"Yes, Ma'am. For instance, Your Ladyship, you want to become a member of the parliament. That poor girl over there was a prostitute until yesterday. I just know these things."

"Do you want to stay here?" Farrokhlaqa asked with anticipation.

"Of course," Munis answered. "Unfortunately it is still not a time for a woman to travel by herself. She must either become invisible, or stay cooped up in a house. My problem is that I can no longer remain housebound, but I have to, because I am a woman. Perhaps I can make a little progress at a time. But then I will have to be stuck in a house for a while. Maybe this is the only way I can see the world, at a snail's pace. That is why I gratefully accept your invitation."

Farrokhlaqa was overjoyed. "Ladies," she addressed the group, "I want to make additions to the villa. There is the gardener who can also do construction work. He is the only male we're going to keep around. We'll start work as soon as possible."

"That's a great idea," declared Munis. "I knew this earlier. I predict success."

Turning to Fa'iza, who was still sobbing, Farrokhlaqa said consolingly, "Don't worry. It is possible to live without virginity. I have lived without it for thirty-three years."

"What will happen to my reputation?" Fa'iza answered dejectedly. "How can I justify it to my husband on wedding night?"

"If it comes to that," Munis said, "I will do something so your husband won't find out. You know me; I'm the one that changes the shape of my face."

"So why didn't you do something to prevent the assault by those monsters from the truck?" Fa'iza asked with an accusatory tone.

"My dear," Munis said, with her temper rising. "I have died and come back to life twice. I see things in a different way. God knows I would fly if I had wings. But my spirit is still earthbound. Believe me, virginity will be of no consequence. Should you find a husband, I'll arrange it so that you will live in conjugal bliss ever after."

Fa'iza calmed down and turned quiet. Waiting for furniture and building supplies to arrive, the women shared their life stories with one another.

Farrokhlaqa's Garden

Part Two

BY SPRING THE GARDEN HAD TURNED into a flower grove. The gardener was right; he did have a green thumb. All he did was touch a bush and it blossomed into a hundred flowers the following week.

They renovated the house together. Farrokhlaqa did not engage in the work per se, but she constantly moved around giving orders and checking details. It took the autumn months to complete the work. The gardener had the women do different building chores: Zarrinko-lah would prepare the mortar; Munis would take it to the building; Fa'iza would carry bricks in a wheelbarrow, while the gardener did the actual construction work. At the end of the autumn the house had six rooms, three showers, and three bathrooms.

On sunny days Farrokhlaqa would rest by the pool and survey with satisfaction the work in progress. Sometimes she would have Zarrinkolah accompany her on her shopping trips to the city. She had a sense of accomplishment in the fact that the project was progressing according to her plans.

When the remodeling work was completed at the end of the autumn, Farrokhlaqa assigned one room to Fa'iza and Munis, who by now had become her primary companions and counselors. Fa'iza tended the kitchen and Munis the other household affairs. She herself took over furnishing and decorating the house. The gardener asked for and received permission to build a small lodge for himself at the far end of the property near the river. He also asked that Zarrinkolah be allowed to assist him in the endeavor.

In due course the gardener built the lodge on the riverbank directly facing the Mahdokht tree—which still had not sprouted limbs and leaves. The barrenness had caused Farrokhlaqa some concern, but the gardener had assured her that it would be full of blooms by the spring. He had also suggested that the human-tree is not like other trees; it needs human breast milk to achieve maturity and growth. Farrokhlaqa was stumped by the suggestion, not being able to think of a source for human breast milk.

"Don't worry," the gardener said, "I am going to marry Zarrinkolah. She will lactate when she bears a child. We will fertilize the tree with her milk."

Fa'iza proposed inviting a cleric to solemnize the marriage. The gardener did not agree; he would perform the ceremony himself without the benefit of the clergy. To Fa'iza, such a marriage was not legitimate. Munis stayed out of the discussion and made no references to her own mind-reading ability. Farrokhlaqa was neutral. She did not care one way or other, as long as there was breast milk to feed the tree, as the gardener had promised.

Zarrinkolah spent most of her time alongside the gardener helping him in his work. He had taught her bricklaying, tree planting, landscaping, cooking, and embroidery. She was always humming as she moved from place to place on the property, something that annoyed Fa'iza, who held Zarrinkolah in low esteem for lax morals and incessant jollity, as if she had to laugh to prove she was alive. Fa'iza had little tolerance for people like that, although she did not let that interfere with her general satisfaction with her current situation. Occasionally she felt a tinge of sadness when she thought of Amir Khan. Deep down she nursed a longing to be married to him, not so much out of love for him but a desire for vindication. To have him as a husband would vindicate her womanhood.

Farrokhlaqa persisted in her plans to become a member of the parliament. Impatiently, she waited for the completion of the building renovations so she could start entertaining celebrities and influential people to cultivate associations with them. In consultations with Munis she had arrived at the conclusion that to have name recognition she had to write poetry and publish it in newspapers and magazines. She was intrigued by the idea and spent much of her time trying to write poems.

At the onset of winter, the house was ready to be fully occupied by the women. Farrokhlaqa furnished the parlor as a music-cum-party room, equipped with comfortable furniture, chandeliers, and bookshelves displaying dozens of poetry anthologies that she had ordered from a bookstore. She bought large candlesticks displaying designs of moths as if they were burned by the flame of the candles, giving poignancy to the timeless metaphor. She also stocked the cellar with various vintages of wines and liquors to ensure an inexhaustible supply for the parties.

Then came the task of developing guest lists and sending invitations. Guests were welcome to arrive Friday mornings and stay well into the early hours of the next day. Lambs were slaughtered and carefully dressed on the premises every Friday morning by the local butcher and sent to the kitchen to be prepared into elaborate dishes overseen by Munis and Fa'iza. Zarrinkolah tended to the lesser details of the process. Soon the word of Farrokhlaqa's hospitality spread among her friends and new acquaintances who would arrive at the villa in large numbers on Fridays. She did not mention a word about the tree to the guests, under orders from the gardener, who wanted to wait for it to be in full bloom later in the year.

Zarrinkolah stopped coming to the house. She spent all her time at the lodge. When Munis brought it up with the gardener, he said that every dawn both of them looked for dewdrops on vegetation to irrigate the tree.

Since Zarrinkolah did not have a baby yet, she could not provide breast milk.

Munis was not able to penetrate the gardener's mind to know his thoughts. She simply asked to join him and his wife in their search for dewdrops. The gardener agreed and the three of them spent the morning hours collecting dewdrops with which the gardener irrigated the tree according to his secret process.

By early April the tree was covered with blooms. It accompanied the chirping birds by singing a haunting song. Farrokhlaqa could not wait to show it off to her guests, but the gardener still would not permit it. "It is not the right time for it yet," he would say gravely. In fact Farrokhlaqa herself was discouraged from visiting the tree. She resented the restriction, although she kept it to herself, afraid of alienating the gardener whom she desperately needed. Besides, she was too busy trying to write poetry, since the Friday morning guests now included a coterie of reporters, poets, painters, novelists, and photographers and she felt the need to produce something to break into their circle. During the hours of leisure Munis would give her comfort and encouragement in her effort to write poetry. Fa'iza was pessimistic about the prospects, but, afraid that Munis would read her mind, she did not think much about it. Sometimes, when she was far enough away from Munis and confidant that distance would insulate her mind against Munis's intrusions, she thought of the enterprise as stupid and blamed the round-faced Munis for creating the delusion in Farrokhlaqa that she could become a poet. Fa'iza recognized that Munis had certain abilities, including reading minds and elongating her face, yet she was born with a round face, therefore she could not escape her simple-mindedness and low-grade intelligence.

April had come to an end and Farrokhlaqa had not yet written a poem.

One Friday morning there was an unexpectedly large influx of guests at the villa, much larger than ever before, somewhere near one hundred people. In her frenzy, Farrokhlaqa put Munis and Fa'iza to work and started desperately looking for Zarrinkolah. She felt a rush of resentment toward her for not pulling her weight, not earning her keep. Then she suddenly saw the gardener among the crowd.

"For God's sake," she yelled at him, "tell your wife to come and give the women a hand in the kitchen. They are crushed under the pressure of work."

"That's not possible," said the gardener calmly. "She became pregnant last night and she is not supposed to move for the next nine months."

"You idiot!" she burst out in a fit of anger. "First of all, how do you know she became pregnant last night? Secondly, what the hell am I going to do with all these guests?"

"Don't fret," said the gardener, unperturbed. "I will have the tree sing. That will calm them, and make them forget their hunger. You can keep the food for yourself. Also, do not invite any more guests until you have produced some poetry. What is the use of them imposing on your hospitality without doing you any good?"

As soon as the gardener left, singing could be heard in the garden. The guests fell silent, transfixed where they were. It was as if they were all encased in a drop of water the size of an ocean. Slowly seeping through the layers of the earth, the drop joined a myriad of elements at the earth's inner core in a dance, a perpetual, harmonic movement with no beginning or end. It was simultaneously slow and rapid. The guests' arms lifted and began to swing overhead, hanging like ropes from the sky, moving so quickly they appeared as a shadow.

"Notice how much sky is around us," Munis whispered in Farrokhlaqa's ear. "There is a sky within a sky, within a sky . . ." Farrokhlaqa noted that the woman had closed her eyes, as if gazing at a distant horizon behind her eyelids. Farrokhlaqa crossed her legs and with a peculiar delight surveyed her guests, who were dazed by their experience and trying to understand it.

Then a green mist set in, engulfing everything and everyone—one color of the rainbow dominating all other colors. All who were present were dissolved into the mist, and then dripped like dewdrops from the tip of a leaf.

At nightfall the tree stopped singing. The guests left the garden noiselessly, wordlessly, entranced by the song they had heard.

Farrokhlaqa stopped inviting guests to the villa. She vowed not to invite anyone until she had written some poetry. She would confine herself to the music room all day and try to compose verse. Munis spent most of her time with the gardener and his wife, who from the beginning of her pregnancy had stopped speaking. She would sit by the window and watch the river silently. Munis and the gardener continued to collect dewdrops to irrigate the tree, as they diligently cared for Zarrinkolah in her delicate condition. As her pregnancy advanced and the contour of her body changed, Zarrinkolah became increasingly translucent, like crystal, with light shining through her. Munis would sometimes look at the river through her as she sat by the window watching the currents.

At the other end of the garden Fa'iza had been left alone. There were no more guests to cook for and receive compliments from on her culinary skills. Farrokhlaqa kept herself in isolation in the music room. Munis had practically moved to the gardener's lodge and rarely stayed in the villa. Fa'iza could not have a conversation even with the gardener, as he was always busy doing something. She felt lonely and desolate. Occasionally she would get dressed and take a day trip to Tehran. In those excursions she would meander past Amir Khan's house. On chance encounters, they would acknowledge each other only by a nod of the head.

It was late September when Farrokhlaqa felt she had gained some virtuosity in manipulating rhyme and rhythm in her poetry. She emerged from the room and sat on the bedstead near the pool. She called to Munis, who was watering the flowerbeds, to listen to her latest composition.

"Munis dear," she said, "this is not really a poem as such, but I think if I continue to work on it, I will have a real one in a couple of years." Munis encouraged her to read it.

"Like I said," Farrokhlaqa demurred, "this is not really a poem, just an experiment with rhyme and meter." Munis insisted.

Flushed with a mixture of excitement and diffidence, Farrokhlaqa began the recitation:

"O sugar bowl, of sugar deprived, O anvil without a
  cobbler
O mirthless laughter, O wall climber who art a
  wobbler
O angel jocund, O giver of justice, serpent-hearted,
  beach-combing
O coquettish one, fairy-like, or a pigeon homing
O thou of shattered wing and broken claw
O giver of comfort, all goodness and no flaw.
Didst thou pack, leave, and not see
In the mirror of thy heart a picture of poor me?
What to expect of this sorrow-laden abode of the
  insane?
What to tell the lifeless simian remains of the one in
  pain?
A sadness covers my heart, say not again of war;
O generous one, tell my heart to beat no more.
Faris'* heart is depressed as a ruined temple,
Longing for the beloved, pure and simple."

* A nickname for "Farrokhlaqa," here a *nom de plume*, occurring in the last couplet of the poem, a common practice in the Iranian classical poetic tradition.

Farrokhlaqa fell silent, looking anxiously at Munis, who lowered her head, staring at her toes. Farrokhlaqa broke the awkward silence.

"What do you think?" she asked. "I know it is full of problems and infelicities. But I have never written a poem. This is my first completed one."

"Let me read it myself," Munis said finally. "I don't quite understand it this way."

Farrokhlaqa gave her the sheet of paper. Munis began reading silently, with concentrated attention. Farrokhlaqa was frantic with anticipation. She didn't think much of Munis as a poetry critic, but she was a reader after all and had some literary sensitivities. In her anxiety Farrokhlaqa flitted her glance from the pool to the trees and from the trees to the pool.

"Excuse me," Munis finally said, "Why do you begin the poem with 'sugar bowl, of sugar deprived?'"

As if expecting the question, Farrokhlaqa beamed with a smile. "You see," she said, " I am fascinated with objects and I have looked at sugar bowls often. Don't you think an empty sugar bowl looks very sad?" Munis nodded in agreement. "That may be so," she went on. "But 'an anvil without a cobbler' sounds strange. Isn't an anvil associated with blacksmiths?"

Farrokhlaqa was taken aback by the observation. She wanted to argue the point but she wasn't quite sure herself.

"Are you certain?" she asked.

"As far as I know," Munis answered.

"So what is the term for the one used by cobblers?"

Munis could not think of it, despite her fairly extensive vocabulary.

"If I change it to 'blacksmith,'" Farrokhlaqa mused, "the whole structure of the poem will shift."

"That may not be a bad thing," Munis said. "The way it is, some of the rhymes don't make sense. Perhaps you can restructure the poem around the concept of 'blacksmith.' Some of the other concepts, for instance 'serpent-hearted' or 'simian remains,' do catch the reader's attention, but they don't make much sense. Perhaps they'll fit better with 'blacksmith.'"

Farrokhlaqa's morale was already undermined. Munis could see that Farrokhlaqa was seeing in her mind's eye the destruction of her dream castle brick-by-brick.

"Don't fret too much about poetry," Munis said sympathetically. "There are other means of success. I'm thinking of the painter who visited here last time. I can see that he is dying to paint a portrait of you. Let him do it and then pay him generously. The word will get around and catch the attention of the movers and shakers. You are already connected with some of them. Just approach them sincerely and tell them you want to be in the parliament. They'll help you."

Munis sensed that Farrokhlaqa had stopped taking down her dream castle and was already considering the proposed strategy.

"I think I'll start a new series of parties from next week," she said resolutely. "I will call up Mosayeb and Ahmad as we'll need man servants to do the work."

As planned, the parties started the following week. Gradually relatives began showing up among the guests, including Amir Khan, who came under the pretext of visiting his sister. He was subdued and restrained—and unaccompanied by his wife.

"Why didn't you bring your wife?" Fa'iza asked pointedly.

"She is too busy," he said. "Besides, she is not into socializing. She is a homemaker, born to keep house."

"I can't say I approve of full-time homemakers," Fa'iza returned. "A woman must have a social dimension, to help her man advance socially. One can't get stuck in the kitchen corner. For example, you don't plan to remain a low-grade employee forever. You want to advance yourself to higher positions in your organization. The way to do it is to network with important people. I have lost count of the number of important people I've gotten to know so far. I just have to drop a hint and any problems I may have will be taken care of."

"Do you happen to know Mr. Atrchian?" asked Amir Khan, brimming with anticipation, "the one who was here last week? You know, bald, short, his face always flushed?"

"Of course," she answered emphatically, insinuating a need for confidentiality. "He and Mr. Manaqebi smoke opium together."

Amir Khan seemed delighted with the answer. He had brought up the man's name with Fa'iza before. But pointedly she never asked why he was interested; she did not want to serve as a go-between.

Farrokhlaqa had agreed to model for the painter. In

addition to Fridays he also came on Tuesdays to work on the portrait. The plan was to have an exhibition, richly financed by Farrokhlaqa, consisting of various sketches the painter had made of her in preparation for the portrait.

Munis continued to spend most of the day at the end of the garden helping the gardener collect dewdrops for the tree. Mosayeb and Ahmad took full charge of the kitchen, obviating the need for the women in catering chores. With the approach of the winter season Farrokhlaqa was thinking of getting rid of the women. Now she knew how to manage her affairs. The exhibition was to open in late January, and she was thinking of leasing a house in Tehran. The garden in Karadj would be her summer residence. She saw no place for women in this scheme.

One night in mid-January the garden was flooded with a mysterious luminescence. Munis, who was sleeping close to the window in the villa, was awakened by it. "She is giving birth," she muttered to herself. Hurriedly, she put on some clothes and headed for the lodge. A heavy snow had fallen through the night and had covered the garden, diffusing the light in all directions, as though the whole universe was aglow.

Zarrinkolah was now a figure of clear crystal, refracting the light in many colors. The gardener, seemingly unconcerned, was sitting on the floor mending his slippers.

"We must help her," Munis yelled at him.

"She does not need help," said the gardener. "A true woman gives birth by herself."

Just before dawn a morning glory came into the world.

The gardener gathered it in his cupped hands and headed toward the riverbank, where he had already dug a small pit in the sand. It was full of frozen snow. Gently, he placed the seedling on the ice.

"It's going to freeze," groaned Munis.

"It will not die. It will grow roots and prosper."

They returned to the room. Zarrinkolah was sitting silently in the middle of her bed. She was no longer crystalline. She had turned into her former self, her breasts swollen with milk. The gardener embraced her tenderly. He kissed her forehead and her hands, gently stroking her hair. He then bent down and massaged her feet.

"We must now feed the tree," said the gardener solemnly, handing a cup to his wife. She expressed her milk in the cup, filling it to the brim.

"Now, go to sleep," he said to his wife, "a restful sleep."

He picked up the cup and with Munis walked to the tree. Turning to Munis, he said, "It is frozen into a sleep. It is good that it is hibernating. By the spring it will be a tree like you've never seen before."

Drop by drop, he spread the milk around the trunk of the tree. By the time he finished, the sun had risen and they returned to the lodge. Munis picked her way slowly through the wintry garden toward the house. She had a sense that she had died again, since nothing seemed strange to her anymore. Somewhere along the way she stopped by a tree and leaned her head against its rough trunk. "I need help," she told herself.

In a way, she envied the prostitute. The prostitute had won too easily, having achieved the sanctity of light, as spontaneously and effortlessly as laughing. Munis could not penetrate this mystery.

"How can I turn into light?" she moaned.

There was no answer.

She lacked the potential to become a tree; it wasn't in her nature. She was not fertile either. She knew that she was rotting from within. She knew that what led to the clarity of light was love, something she had never experienced in her life. She had progressed to the edge of wonderment, but love was oceans away. She knew that love would come if she could sincerely feel the essence of a tree past the roughness of its bark. But always, the physical sensation of the roughness interrupted her. She always knew the malice of humankind, without herself being in its possession. She had not learned to be malicious. She only knew malice.

In a deserted stretch of the Karadj highway Munis had come face-to-face with unbridled lust, although she knew what lust was before being touched by it. The problem was that she had an unbounded awareness of things, an awareness that instilled undue caution in her, making her fearful that action would lead to ignominy, humiliation. This created in her a desire to be ordinary, average. Yet she did not truly know what it meant to be ordinary. She did not know that it meant not loving an earthworm, not genuflecting at the altar of withered leaves, not standing in prayer at the call of a lark, not climbing a mountain to see the sunrise, not staying awake all night to gaze at the Ursa Major. She did not differentiate between earth and gravel, but she distinguished the earth from the sky. She had not seen the skies of the earth, but she knew there were earths of the sky. She saw herself in an inevitable process of stagnation. She was already partially rotten within.

"What can I do with this mass of trivial knowledge?" she wondered aloud. "How can I cut through it?"

Farrokhlaqa was awake and standing at the entrance to the house in her woolen housecoat.

"The house is freezing cold," she said, sounding upset. "Obviously, you left the door open."

"I'm sorry," said Munis, already aware that Farrokhlaqa wanted the women out of the house.

"In your opinion," Munis asked, "what can I do with all this trivial knowledge?"

"What trivial knowledge?" Farrokhlaqa asked, puzzled.

"I mean all this trivial knowledge, for example, you wanting us out of the house. Why should I know this?"

Farrokhlaqa shrugged her shoulders dismissively. By now she had learned how to deal with Munis and was no longer intimidated by her mind-reading ability. She had decided that Munis was too simple-minded to be able to exploit the knowledge she gained from mind reading for some practical purpose. She was only tormented by it.

"I'm going to Tehran today," she announced. "I have rented a house there. You people can stay here for as long as you want. I'm going to be back in the summer. Give the key to the gardener when you leave."

Mahdokht

(Reprise)

MAHDOKHT HAD PLANTED HERSELF on the riverbank in the fall. She suffered as the clay around her ankles hardened. The freezing rainstorms of the season tore her clothes to shreds. She was left dressed in tatters. She shivered incessantly until the winter frost froze her all over. But her eyes were left open, looking at the river as it flowed by.

With the first spring showers, a thaw set in and splintered the ice and she felt the tingling of sprouting buds on her limbs. Her toes resumed their growth as roots, and they penetrated deeper and deeper into the earth. She could hear them grow. They extracted nutrients from the earth and spread them through her organs. She listened to the sound of the roots and watched the water in the river turn green.

The fall arrived again, and with it came the cold. But she no longer suffered. The roots stopped their growth and so did every part of her body.

That winter she was fed with dewdrops. Although she felt the frost covering her, she still saw the river as green, with a slight tinge of blue.

In the spring she was once more covered with sprouting buds. She welcomed the spring and her heart filled with joy, a joy that she passed on to the buds as they grew into green leaves.

When the summer arrived, she saw the water turn blue and schools of fish in it.

Freezing weather returned in early autumn and the sky darkened. But her heart was still joyful, having now found unison with the spirit of the tree, storing all the goodness of the earth.

By midwinter she was being fed with human breast milk. This gave her an explosive burst of energy thawing the ice even before the advent of spring. But it also made her ache all over as she had to confine the force within her body. Now, as she stared at the river, she no longer saw a continual stream, but a flux of liquid drops rushing in the riverbed helter-skelter in their numberless multitude. This exacerbated her pain. Her senses infiltrated the droplets of the river current and made her palpitate in unison with the heartbeat of each drop.

She was fed human milk for three months. Toward the end of April the pressure within her had reached explosive force. It burst out suddenly and violently. Although it was an explosion, it was not an instantaneous blowout; it was nuanced and in stages. It was as if her tissues were coming apart slowly and jarringly. In a perpetual transmutation Mahdokht was separating from herself, suffering excruciating, unbearable pain like birth contractions, almost causing her eyes to burst out of their sockets. The water was no longer a mass of droplets but fractured into infinite tiny bits of atoms of ether.

It all came to a sudden end. The tree was now a mountain of seeds. A strong wind scattered them into the river. The seeds traveled with the water to all corners of the world.

Fa'iza

(Reprise)

DURING AUTUMN THE CITY AIR was fresh. By late morning it was pleasant to take a walk in the streets. Almost every morning around eleven Fa'iza met Amir Khan for a stroll. She would arrive in Victory Square on the bus from Karadj and he would be there to meet her. He often grumbled about his wife and she listened patiently. The wife was slovenly, he complained, and didn't know how to cook. She couldn't even take proper care of their baby. Fa'iza sympathized with him and tried to give him helpful advice.

A month into their assignations, the company where Amir Khan worked penalized him for excessive absences. This was a blow to him, and he had to change the time of their meetings to five in the afternoon. Now she would arrive from Karadj in late afternoon to meet Amir Khan. They would meander the streets near Victory Square and talk. Sometimes they would take in a movie or have dinner in a restaurant. After a while, it was apparent that the routine was becoming monotonous. Besides, they were running out of things to talk about.

"I don't know how to put this," Amir Khan said one day, "but it is not a good thing for you to commute from Karadj every day. I'm afraid something might happen to you. A woman shouldn't be traveling by herself late at night."

"What should we do?" she asked.

"Why don't you come back and live in Tehran?"

"Where? In whose house?"

"Go back to your grandmother."

"What makes you think she'll take me back? She doesn't understand our lifestyle. She'd think something bad has happened to me and be even more strict than before."

Amir Khan thought for a moment. "Perhaps it is better if I rent you a room," he said.

"Shame on you," Fa'iza objected diffidently. "What makes you think I'm that kind of girl?"

"What if we enter into a concubinage?"* Amir Khan proposed. "That will at least formalize our relationship."

Fa'iza disliked the term "concubine" applying to her, but said nothing.

* In some Islamic communities relationships with so-called concubines are religiously sanctioned and are considered common-law marriages.

They went to see a notary public one afternoon. "We do not handle concubinage," said the registrar, "only permanent marriages."

They went through the formalities and registered their marriage with the understanding that there would be no announcements until Amir Khan had prepared his wife for a separation. They spent the night in a hotel room.

The morning after, Amir Khan woke up in a depressed mood. He kept moving around the room looking for things. Fa'iza, for her part, ignored him as he stood in front of the window gazing at the street below. He felt his life was in a shambles and he had no one to complain to.

"We must look for a small house," Fa'iza broke the silence.

"Wait a minute," barked Amir Khan. "I'm taking you to my own house."

"Over my dead body!" she retorted. "What makes you think I'm going to live under one roof with another wife of yours? No way!"

Fa'iza started looking for a place to live and soon found a place on Salsabil Avenue. Amir Khan looked for and found a new job at a trading company to support two households, still hoping that Fa'iza would put him in contact with Mr. Atrchian.

Life goes on for the two of them—not ideally, but not too badly either.

Munis

(Reprise)

MUNIS STAYED BEHIND to help the gardener for three months. Together they nurtured the tree with the milk from Zarrinkolah's breasts. In the middle month of the spring the tree was adorned with magnificent flowers in bloom. One morning they found that the tree had turned into a huge mound of seeds. A wind came and scattered the seeds on the river.

"Munis," the gardener addressed her in a serious tone, "it is time for you to become human."

"But I want to turn into pure light," Munis told him. "How do I become light?"

"The day you conceive the essence of darkness," he answered. "That is what you have to comprehend.

That is the principle. Don't seek to become light; that is a journey of no return. Look at our mutual friend: she wanted to become a tree and she achieved her aim. She thought it would be difficult, but it was not. Sadly, she did not achieve humanity. Now as seed, she will have to restart the journey toward humanity, a journey that will take eons.

"Now I tell you to go in search of darkness anew. Descend to the depths, to the depth of depths. There you will see the light aglow in your hands, by your side. That is being human. Now, go become human."

In an instant Munis turned into a tiny whirlwind and rose to the sky in a cloud of dust. She was then in the desert, an endless desert.

Seven years passed and she passed through seven deserts, fatigued and aged, devoid of hope and vision, but replete with experience. That was all.

She arrived in the city after seven years. She bathed, put on fresh clothes, and became a simple schoolteacher.

Farrokhlaqa Sadroddin Golchehreh

(Reprise)

ALL WINTER FARROKHLAQA STAYED in the house she
had rented in the city. The portraitist was almost a con-
tinuous presence in the house. He was twenty-five years
old and full of dreams for his art—which he shared with
Farrokhlaqa. An exhibition of his portrait and sketches of
Farrokhlaqa had been held. A large crowd of admirers and
cognoscenti had turned up on the opening night, prais-
ing the works on display. But attendance had dropped
drastically the following days and the young painter was
devastated. Farrokhlaqa spent all winter trying to build
up his self-esteem. But by the spring she was tired of his
whining. She gave him some money to go to Paris and
train with great masters.

In the absence of the painter Farrokhlaqa felt lonely and bored. She thought of returning to the garden, but she did not think she could stand the women.

Mr. Merrikhi paid her a visit one day. He was an old friend of Fakhroddin Azod and privy to her affair with him. He was very respectful, reverential in fact, toward her. He believed she had a remarkable potential for social advancement, except that it had not been channeled in the right direction. He proposed marriage to open new venues for her to achieve her goals. She consented.

They both made progress. Merrikhi went to the parliament. Farrokhlaqa got involved in charitable activities. He was awarded a medal for meritorious service. She became the honorary head of an orphanage. He was appointed to a foreign-service post in Europe. She went with him.

They have a fairly good relationship, not torrid by any means, but not frigid either.

Zarrinkolah

(Reprise)

ZARRINKOLAH MARRIED KIND GARDENER and became pregnant. In time, she gave birth to a morning glory. She loved it as her own child. The morning glory flourished on the bank of the river.

"Zarrinkolah," her husband called to her, "we must go on a journey."

Zarrinkolah cleaned the house and packed a bundle of clothing for the journey.

"But we don't need clothes where we're going," her husband said. "Leave your bundle behind." She obeyed, and took her husband by the hand.

They embraced the morning glory. The morning glory wrapped its foliage around them and they all rose to the sky in a puff of smoke.

Author's Note

WHEN I WAS AN EIGHT- OR NINE-YEAR-OLD GIRL, my mother and I raced each other to finish reading books. It was our favorite leisure activity. There was a small thrift store around the corner from our home in Tehran that sold trinkets and things. The shop owner, Mr. Roshan, also repaired women's hosiery, a newly available luxury item, which was too costly to throw out after the first run (we are talking the early 1950s here). Mr. Roshan also had several rows of books that people could rent for about a penny per night. I would go there and rent two books, one for myself and one for my mother. We read the books quickly and then swapped them.

Translated by Shahbaz Parsipour

Most of these books were from France. For the book covers, the Iranian publisher had used pictures of actors from the movies that were based on the books. I have forgotten the names of these actors, but their beauty, as well as their expensive clothes, affected me deeply in those years.

We also read American detective stories. That is why one name has been etched in my mind since childhood: Jack Smith. I cannot recall whether this Jack Smith was a policeman, a detective, or maybe even a criminal. But the name stayed in my mind so stubbornly that for years before I came to the US, whenever anyone spoke of America, the name Jack Smith would instantly pop up in my mind.

My mother was in her early thirties at the time. For a while she ordered my brothers, Shahram and Shahriar, and me to kiss her hand every morning, and to greet her with, "Good morning Dear Princess!" She was from the Qajar dynasty, a descendent of the kings of that house, but the sad yet funny aspect of our life at that time was that we were living in a single room in my grandmother's very old house. We were extremely poor and our dinner consisted of only bread and milk for nearly a year. This was very little food for me, and especially for Shahram, who had just recovered from typhoid.

Father, who had quit working for the Ministry of Justice as a judge, had left us in utter poverty to travel to the south of the country, hoping to try his luck there as a lawyer. And since Mother did not have money to socialize, she contented herself by reading books about French chivalry and American crime. And of course she was also happy when we kissed her hand and called her Dear Princess. But that didn't last long. We carried out our duty for only a week perhaps and then, laughing and joking, we stopped altogether.

Mother was an outgoing and quirky woman. "Come and record my voice," she once suggested to my brother Shahriar, years later, "so that when I die and people attend my funeral, you'll play the tape at the end of the service. I'd like to thank everybody for having done me the favor of attending the ceremonies."

"But my *shajun*," responded Shahriar, "some people may just be scared to death if we do that!"

Shajun was the title our mother had given to herself. In the Persian language, shah means "king" and *jun* or *jan* means "dear." *Shah-zadeh* means "prince" or "princess," but the *zadeh* usually gets dropped. And so at moments, she was still Dear Princess.

"If I were Mrs. Fakhrodoleh," Mother often said, "then I'd know what to do with my money!" Mrs. Fakhrodoleh was a wealthy woman, also of the Qajars, who had performed important social services, including building a hospital for the poor.

So, I knew a number of things about my mother. One, she loved to sit on the bed as if it were a throne. Two, she was an imaginative person, and considered herself very important in her own daydreams. Three, she loved literature and read a lot of books, although she was unable to write poetry as her mother and stepsister did. And last but not least, she loved another man instead of my father.

— 117 —

"I'd have divorced your father," she would tell me on an almost daily basis, "if you weren't around!"

That remark has caused me a great deal of psychological pain. I suffer from shyness. For years, I thought that I might have done a great favor to my mother if I were not born. These feelings propelled me to try to get away from my aristocratic family when I was older, and I became a socialist. Yet when I began to write *Women Without Men*, my mother's characteristics were gradually woven into the character called Farrokhlaqa Sadroddin Golchehreh. This character is actually somewhat based on a cousin of mine as well as my mother. My cousin, also a very beautiful woman, decided suddenly to become a poet at the age of thirty-seven. Becoming a poet has become a common practice in Iran. People, without knowing anything about the rules of poetry, put words together abruptly and, using weird thoughts, believe they are creating poetry.

For example, "Light's affection is running in electric wires," or "The scream coming to the surface of existence was violet in color," or "Earth's Red told the Blue of Presence: I don't like destiny." And so on. Some of these poems are interesting, but they become ridiculous when, in order to cover their own illiteracy, some poets claim that the grammatical conventions in poetry are nonsense and have to be discarded altogether.

Is this desire to throw out the old the reason why millions of people poured into the streets and kicked the Shah out without understanding what could happen next? The new government turned on them and their loved ones, executing hundreds of thousands, even their own teenagers, who wanted to create a new government.

Anyway, my cousin was one of those who decided to write poetry. Years later, she stopped just as suddenly because she was suffering from extreme breathing difficulties, which eventually caused her death. I knitted the personalities of my mother and my cousin together to help me create the personality of Mrs. Farrokhlaqa Sadroddin Golchehreh.

I chose "Farrokhlaqa" because it is the name of an extremely beautiful woman in Iranian mythical stories. She is one of the main characters in a famous story, "Amir Arsalan Namdar" (The Famous Prince Arsalan), which is a long tale once told by an ancestor of mine named Naqibol-mamalek (known as Naqib). He recited the story in a loud voice for a Qajar king of Iran, while one of the king's daughters wrote it down. The tale tells of the love of a young Roman named Amir Arsalan, for Farrokhlaqa, the daughter of King Petrous. Of course Naqib's notion of Rome was more like today's Turkey, which, in fact, used to be called "The Eastern Rome" in Iran.

Many of the other characters in this book were inspired by people I knew. There is the character I named Zarrinkolah (Golden Hat). One day, when going to the local grocery on an errand from my grandmother, I met a very beautiful woman, tall and slender, wearing bright lipstick. There was a strange smile on her face. She was holding a large watermelon in her hands and staring at a constable with a very sexy look in her eyes. It was a look

I had never seen before, even though our house was close to what was then Tehran's official brothel.

I was inspired by that woman's presence and that smile when I was creating Zarrinkolah's character. One day many years later, while I was imprisoned by the leaders of the Islamic Republic, jailed for writing this very book, I walked with a prostitute in the prison's courtyard. She was old and tired, arrested because she was an addict. Since she had no one to come visit her in the prison, and since the prison food was terrible indeed, I shared with her the food that I bought from the prison's store. That day in the courtyard, she told me she was forced into prostitution at the age of ten. Then, as she was walking away from me, she turned back toward me, smiling, and suddenly I knew it was the very same woman I had met as a child. So, my prostitute was now old, an addict, and very lonely.

One of my aunties had been given away at the age of fourteen to a fifty-year-old man in an arranged marriage. She gave birth to two children. After her son died at an early age, she realized that she could not live with her husband anymore, and divorced him. She had learned how to type and was employed in a government office. She was now standing on her own feet but she was very lonely. Living in the brutally traditional, religious Iranian society of those times, she was not allowed to have a boyfriend. So she became a dervish, following a certain old dervish guru. She also tried her hand at writing stories and poetry. I never heard her bad-mouth or gossip about anyone. She gave a portion of her small income to the poor. I mixed her character with parts of myself, and I created Munis.

This aunt had a daughter who was terribly shy. I have never seen anyone like her my entire life. She had a very beautiful and clear voice but being a god-fearing person, she did not sing. She suffered from anorexia during the latter years of her life and when lowered into her grave, she weighed less than sixty pounds. Mahdokht's character is based on her.

Another cousin of mine was a good girl who turned bad unexpectedly. She truly believed that I was an idiot because my face is round. She was right in a way, because she took advantage of me often, and I was deceived every time. She would tell me that if a certain woman saw me, she was going to attack me. Then, when my cousin was sure I would avoid that woman altogether, she would tell her that I had told her husband that she was having secret love affairs. The character of Fa'iza in the book is not really like my cousin, since Fa'iza is deeply in love with a man and my cousin never fell in love, but I always had her in mind when I was creating Fa'iza.

When I was fourteen years old, and very sensitive, as teenagers often are, I went to Karadj with some relatives. I had lived in Tehran all my life and did not have even the slightest clue about village life. At the time, Karadj was a small vacation resort near Tehran. The town had only two or three streets and was surrounded by farms, large and small gardens, and tiny villages.

We went to one of the gardens that belonged to a

wealthy family. It was night and I was lying on a bed in the middle of the garden, watching the full moon in the sky. There were tall trees reaching toward the sky all around me. The weather was cool, much like the climate I would find in northern California years later when I was forced to leave Iran. The way the trees were arranged, and how they seemed separated from the sky and the earth, gave me the impression that I was sleeping on a theater set. People around me were talking but I could not hear them. I was absorbed in the beauty surrounding me. That was why, years later, I had all the women in the book along with The Kind Gardener go to Karadj. Now Karadj has expanded into a frightening, large city and I am not sure if those beautiful gardens still exist.

Everyone who influenced the characters I created in this novella is dead now. Generally, when I think about the people I once knew, I find that the number of dead is far greater than the living. I hope none of those I have described here will be offended in the afterlife, if such a thing exists.

And last but not least, there is no doubt that *Women Without Men* now belongs to Shirin Neshat as much as it does to me.

Shahrnush Parsipur
Richmond, California

The Feminist Press is an independent nonprofit literary publisher that promotes freedom of expression and social justice. We publish exciting writing by women and men who share an activist spirit and a belief in choice and equality. Founded in 1970, we began by rescuing "lost" works by writers such as Zora Neale Hurston and Charlotte Perkins Gilman, and established our publishing program with books by American writers of diverse racial and class backgrounds. Since then we have also been bringing works from around the world to North American readers. We seek out innovative, often surprising books that tell a different story.

See our complete list of books at **feministpress.org**, and join the Friends of FP to receive all our books at a great discount.

THE FEMINIST PRESS
AT THE CITY UNIVERSITY OF NEW YORK
FEMINISTPRESS.ORG